PRAISE FOR DEB

Once again Sprinkle thrills the reader with her masterful plotting. Spellbinding action to the very end with a twist.

— DIANN MILLS, CHRISTY-AWARD WINNING
ROMANTIC SUSPENSE AUTHOR

The Case of the Innocent Husband is a clever and engaging whodunnit in this new series featuring Mackenzie Love and Samantha Majors. Deborah Sprinkle kept me guessing to the very end—I did not see the final twist coming.

— PATRICIA BRADLEY, AUTHOR OF THE
NATCHEZ TRACE PARK RANGERS

THE CASE OF THE
INNOCENT
HUSBAND

a mac & sam
mystery

A NOVEL BY

DEBORAH SPRINKLE

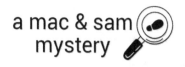

Scrivenings
PRESS
Quench your thirst for story.
www.ScriveningsPress.com

*To Jim,
Thank you for
your sweet
friendship!
Love you!,
Blessings!
Deborah
Sprinkle*

Published by Scrivenings Press LLC
15 Lucky Lane
Morrilton, Arkansas 72110
https://ScriveningsPress.com

Printed in the United States of America

Paperback ISBN 978-1-64917-230-3

eBook ISBN 978-1-64917-231-0

Editors: Erin R. Howard and K. Banks

Cover by Linda Fulkerson - www.bookmarketinggraphics.com

This is a work of fiction. Unless otherwise indicated, all names, characters, businesses, events, and incidents are either the product of the author's imagination or used in a fictitious manner. Any resemblance to actual persons, living or dead, or actual events is purely coincidental.

To God be the glory.

ACKNOWLEDGMENTS

When I start to write about who I want to thank for helping put a book together, I always find it a bit overwhelming. When I say it takes a village, I mean it. How do I express my gratitude and my humility adequately?

I'll begin with my readers, those of you who support my work and ask for the next book. You have no idea how much that means to an author. Thank you.

To my Word Weaver posse, Bonnie Sue Beardsley, Starr Ayers, Denise Holmberg, Linda Dindzans, Caroline Powers, Sandra Vosburgh, and Sandra Melville Hart. What would I do without your monthly critiques? I thank God for all of you!

For Detective Sergeant Steve Sitzes of the Washington Police Department. I can't thank you enough for sharing your expertise with me and helping to make this book as true to life as possible. I take full responsibility for any mistakes in procedure, etc.

For DiAnn Mills, my mentor and my friend. Thank you for always being on the other end of the phone when I need you.

For Linda Fulkerson for making Scrivenings Press what it is, a family of authors who lift each other up, full of support and love. I thank God He directed my books to you.

For Susan Page Davis, my friend, who cared enough to speak the truth when it was needed the most. Thank you from the bottom of my heart.

For the love of my life, my husband of more than 50 years, Les, who not only supports me emotionally, but brings me lunch and dinner so I can write. Along with doing all the household chores. He really is amazing.

To God be the glory.

CHAPTER 1

As Private Investigator Mackenzie Love entered Cowan's Restaurant, eating stopped, and glares from the diners hit her like a barrage of arrows. Her confidence faltered. Should she go somewhere else for breakfast? But what good would that do? It was the same all over town.

Besides, Mac didn't relish the idea of braving the chilly autumn rain again, and here, at least one person was on her side. She closed her umbrella and wiped her damp shoes on the mat.

A plump red-haired server approached with a smile—Ivy, her good friend since grade school, and a welcome sight. "Come on. Don't pay any attention to them." She rolled her eyes. "They'll get over it."

Mac followed her to a corner booth. "Thanks, girlfriend."

"The usual?"

Mac nodded. After Ivy left, she studied the other diners in the restaurant. She'd grown up in Washington, Missouri. These were her friends, her neighbors, the people who'd helped her recover from the death of her parents.

But, when Eleanor Davis was found shot in her garage, Mac's relationship with the townsfolk changed. According to the good citizens of Washington, Connor Davis killed his estranged wife, Eleanor, and that's all there was to it. It didn't matter that twelve men and women of the jury decided there was reasonable doubt. What did they know?

And since Mackenzie discovered the evidence that got Connor Davis acquitted, they put her squarely in the enemy camp. It didn't matter that she was doing her job. As far as they were concerned, Mac should have refused to work for the defense. Never mind a little thing called justice or the fact she had bills to pay.

She straightened and smiled at a neighbor—who averted her eyes.

After college, there was never any question in Mac's mind about where she wanted to live. She headed home as fast as she could. But now ... would they get over it?

Until Mac caught the actual killer, most of her friends and neighbors would have trouble letting go of their original verdict. She flexed her shoulders. Therefore, her single-minded goal became to find who shot Eleanor Davis.

Or she'd have to move.

Finding Eleanor's killer would be a daunting task. She sighed. Eliminating Connor left no other suspects, and, judging from her reception this morning, she wouldn't get much help from the community.

Mac surveyed the patrons again. Her skin itched from darted looks of animosity, but she remained outwardly relaxed. "Never let them see you sweat." That's what her daddy always said.

The door chimed open and a petite woman stepped in. She removed the hood of her raincoat and looked around. When her sparkling blue eyes lit on Mac, a broad smile spread across her face.

"There you are." Samantha Masters strode across the room, smiling and nodding to acquaintances—seemingly impervious to the icy stares and murmured epithets.

"What's up, partner?" Mac relaxed at the sight of her friend.

"I tried calling but got no answer."

Mac pulled her phone from her purse. "Sorry. It's on vibrate. Want a coffee?"

"No time." She tugged on Mac's arm. "Come on. We have a lead."

The day seemed to brighten. Maybe they were finally getting somewhere.

At the door, Mac turned. "Have a nice day, everyone." She exited before any rude replies dampened her mood. "Kill them with kindness." That's what her mama always said.

On the sidewalk, Mac opened her umbrella. "Meet you at the office, partner." She dashed for her car. This lead could be the break they needed.

The office of Mackenzie Love and Samantha Majors, Private Investigators, was at the corner of Second and Johnson, a quaint little house they'd purchased from Mac's uncle's estate. After renovations, the living room, dining room, and kitchen became one long room on one side, with two offices separated by a bath on the other.

What was once the living room served as their reception area—not that they ever had any clients that had to wait. Once, Mackenzie left her office door shut on purpose so her next appointment had to sit down, and she could usher him in. It was a pleasant sensation, but she felt too guilty to ever do it again.

The two former bedrooms worked well as offices for

Samantha and Mackenzie. Samantha's was pale yellow, with Danish modern-style furniture she bought at the second-hand store in the next town. Mackenzie preferred a soothing green color on her walls and oak furniture.

Her wooden desk came from the bank when they upgraded to metal ones. She wasn't sure but believed it to be about seventy-five years old. The drawers tended to stick, and she kept a bar of soap handy to use on the runners.

As they came through the front door, Mac hesitated. A man sat in the reception area. "Did we have an appointment today?" she said to Sam in a low voice.

"No. This gentleman is our lead." Sam gestured toward the man with a flourish. "Mr. Reese."

Sam liked a dash of flair now and again, and Mac wouldn't have been surprised if she'd bowed. The man looked as if he was rethinking getting involved with a couple of nutty women. Only he seemed the type to use the word dames.

"Mr. Reese." Mac stuck out her hand. "Thank you for coming."

He rose, and Mac got a better view of him. Overalls, long-sleeve cotton shirt, and well-worn brown boots. Grease ground into every crevice of his hands and nails. A mechanic?

"I heard you was looking into the death of Mrs. Davis." He shoved his hands into his pockets. "She was a nice lady, and I figure if I can help, then it's my duty to tell you what I know."

A tingle of excitement coursed through Mackenzie. Was she about to hear the words that would break this case wide open? "Please, sit down. Would you like some water or a soda?"

He shook his head. "I saw her." He scratched his neck and flashed a look at Mackenzie. "Two days before she died. She was getting on the Thursday train to Kansas City." He sat on the edge of the chair.

Mackenzie and Samantha shared a quick look. Questions flooded her brain. What should she ask first? "You're certain it was Mrs. Davis?"

"Yeah. She worked for my doctor—until she got married. Doc Yancy, but he retired this year. Got a new guy now."

Mac grabbed her notepad. "What time did you see Mrs. Davis get on the train?"

He puffed out his cheeks and squinted at the ceiling. "Saw her pull up about four-thirty, I guess. I was working on Mr. Matthews's car. I own the garage downtown. He'd come back on the noon train, and it wouldn't start. Battery was dead." He shrugged. "I told him I'd take care of it, and I was just finishing up when Mrs. Davis and that man walked past me. I was going to call out to her, but ..."

"A man was with her?" Sam scooted her chair closer to Reese.

"Yeah. It wasn't her husband. I know Connor. This guy was older, with a mustache and beard."

"How did you know he was older?" Mac leaned forward and gave him her full attention.

"His beard." Reese stroked his stubbled chin. "Lots of gray in it."

Sam touched her head. "Could you see his hair?"

"No. He wore a cap. One of those that snap in the front? Don't know what they're called."

"I know the kind." Mac nodded. "A driving or a golf cap. Did you notice anything else about him?"

Reese fiddled with the buttons on his overalls. "No." His eyes widened and he raised his left hand. "Yeah. He was missing half his pinky on his left hand. I saw it when he helped Mrs. Davis onto the train."

"Bravo." Sam clapped. "Now that's something we can work with. Thank you, Mr. Reese."

Mac smiled at her partner's enthusiasm. "Yes, thank you." She turned to the man before them. "But how could you see Mrs. Davis and the man get on the train from the parking lot? Not that I don't believe you. I just want to get the facts straight in my head."

"Mr. Matthews told me to leave his keys with the woman in the gift shop," Reese said. "So, I followed Mrs. Davis and the man to the station. I watched the train board from there."

"That makes sense." Mackenzie smiled. "How about height and weight? For the man."

"Not tall. A couple inches taller than Mrs. Davis." Reese lifted his eyes to the ceiling. "Hard to tell weight with coats and all, but I'd guess medium."

"One eighty, one ninety? Around there?" Mac stood. "About my height?"

Reese nodded.

"Why didn't you go to the police with this information?"

"I got my reasons." He pushed to his feet. "If you have to take it to the cops ..." He shrugged. "But don't bring me into it."

"For now, we'll investigate this on our own." Mac took a step toward the door. "But I can't promise we'll be able to keep you out of it in the future. That's the best I can do."

"At least you're honest." He offered his hand. "Hope it helps."

"Can we contact you later if we have some more questions?" She walked him to the door.

He nodded. "I gave your partner my information."

After their visitor left, Sam perched on the arm of the sofa, her blue eyes dancing with excitement. "What do you think? A love affair gone wrong?"

"Possible." Mackenzie picked up her notepad. She worked best putting random ideas on paper. Older man. Half pinky finger missing left hand. Medium weight and height.

"Put down possible affair," Sam said.

"I'm getting there." Mac scribbled down the information. "If they took the train to Kansas City on Thursday, maybe she came back by train on Saturday."

"The same day Connor found her dead in her garage."

"This is a big breakthrough." Mac plopped into a chair. "The police assumed the overnight bag in her trunk was because she was getting ready to leave, but what if she'd just returned from the train station when someone attacked her?"

"They didn't find a ticket."

"It should have been on her phone," Mac said. "The killer must have deleted it somehow."

"The police techs could have recovered it. There must be another reason. One we're not thinking of." Sam rose and stretched. "I'll see if I can find out what hotel she used in Kansas City."

"There's a lot of them. We'll divide them up."

A knock at the door. Mac raised her eyebrows at her partner. Two people visiting the office in one day? Things were picking up.

"Come in."

Miss Prudence Freebody, Mac's high school chemistry teacher, retired now, stood in the open doorway. Mac's smile froze on her face. The students called her Freezebody because she had a way of looking over her glasses that chilled the blood in a teen's veins. What was she doing here? Had the town sent her to tell Mac to leave?

CHAPTER 2

Mac gaped at her.

"Mackenzie Love, I've come to talk to you." The tall, skeletal woman marched across the room to the reception area. "What do you think you're doing?"

Out of the corner of her eye, Mac caught Sam shrinking into the background. *Thanks a lot, partner.*

"Close your mouth, dear. It's very unbecoming." Miss Freebody placed her purse on an end table. "I haven't spent my precious time teaching you how to reason based on facts just to see you crumble the first time you find your back against a wall."

Anger rose in a rush. "I'm not crumbling, Miss Freezebody. I'm determined to find who killed Eleanor Davis." Mac slapped a hand over her mouth. What had she done?

Miss Freebody cocked an eyebrow at her. Then she chuckled. "You've grown a spine, Mackenzie. Good." The older lady sat down. "Hello, Mrs. Majors."

"Please call me Sam. Short for Samantha."

Mac feared Sam would curtsy, but she stuck out her hand

instead. Sam hadn't had the dubious pleasure of being in Miss Freebody's class. Her family moved to Washington after she graduated from some fancy high school in St. Louis.

"I prefer Samantha," Miss Freebody said. "My name is Prudence. You may call me Miss P."

Mac and Sam exchanged a look. A laugh was in their future, but not now.

"You may or may not know that I was once a forensic scientist with the state," Miss Freebody said. "I still have some connections there, as well as skills in that area."

Was Miss Freebody offering to help with their investigation? Mac glanced at Sam, who looked as confused as she felt.

"I didn't know that," Mac said.

The expectant look on her teacher's face answered Mac's question … Miss Freebody wanted to be asked.

"Would you excuse us a moment?" Mac motioned Sam into her office. "I think she's offering her services. How do you feel about that?"

"I don't know. If we find anything that needs to be examined, shouldn't we give it to the police?"

"Probably." Mac hated to turn her old teacher away. She seemed so eager to help. "She's got a good mind. And, although she was tough, I always knew she cared about us. We could use her to do research. If she's willing."

Sam gazed at the closed office door. "A third perspective wouldn't hurt. Would we pay her? We aren't flush."

"Good question." Mac bit her lip. "I guess we lay it all out and see what she says."

Mac opened the door. "Miss Freebody—" She was gone.

"In here." Miss Freebody called from the kitchen. "I decided to make coffee."

"Sit down, please." Mac took her elbow and steered her to the conference table. "We need to talk."

"Miss Freebody—Miss P." Sam smiled at her. "We'd like you to help us with our case. There are a few minor problems, though."

"Yes?"

"One, we really should turn any evidence we find over to the police immediately." Sam gave a half-shrug of regret. "And two, while we could use someone of your brainpower to help with research, we can't afford to pay you."

"I don't need the money." Miss Freebody waved a dismissive hand in the air. "If you want my help, I'm sure I can work it into my schedule."

Mac and Sam nodded at each other. Miss P officially joined the team.

"Now I'll make us all coffee, and you can bring me up to date on the case."

Mac's mouth went dry. She hoped they hadn't made a big mistake.

"Connor Davis found his estranged wife Eleanor at four in the afternoon laying on the garage floor. She'd been shot." Mac passed a copy of the police file to Miss P. "He immediately called 911, and the police and ambulance were there within ten minutes. Eleanor Davis was pronounced dead at four-twenty that Saturday."

"I heard all that at the trial." Miss P ran a finger down a page as she read. "It seems the only evidence against Mr. Davis was that Eleanor was shot with a nine-millimeter bullet, and he had a gun that used that caliber ammunition. Connor claimed he gave the gun to Eleanor for protection because she was living alone."

"They found the gun in the bushes by the house. It was Connor's," Sam said. "It'd been wiped clean. Even the remaining bullets."

"Plus, Eleanor left an unfinished text that indicated Connor saw her with another man, giving him incentive."

Miss P glanced at the screenshot of the text and furrowed her brow. "I am behind the times."

"And, no one could collaborate Connor's alibi for the time of the shooting." Mac pointed to a line on the page in front of Miss P. "That's where I came in. I found the man who had lunch with him."

"Creating quite a sensation." Miss P raised an eyebrow at Mac. "You need to solve this one posthaste, young lady. Your reputation depends on it."

"Our reputation depends on it." Sam put her arm around Mac's shoulders.

"As far as motive, young Connor was the only one who benefited from his wife's death." Miss P eyed the two women over her glasses. "She stood to inherit a fortune from her father. It was in Connor's best interest to patch up their differences, or—" She drew a finger across her throat. "Get rid of her before she had the chance to divorce him. Especially if there was another man in the picture." She sat back in her chair. "We have a difficult job ahead of us. We must find someone who had as much motive to kill Mrs. Davis as her husband."

Mac and Sam snorted.

"You're going to fit right in, Miss P." Mac patted her arm. "As a matter of fact, we may have another suspect. Mr. Reese told us about a man getting on the train with Eleanor a few days before she died."

"Leonard Reese? He was in the same class as Connor and Eleanor." Miss P removed her glasses and stared past them. "Not a good chemistry student, but excellent with his hands."

Sam snickered. Mac gave her a stern look.

"He owns a garage, I believe." Miss P polished her glasses before replacing them.

"Do you remember every student you ever had in class?" Sam's tone was one of amazement.

"Of course."

"If we could get a rough sketch of our mystery man, do you think you could recognize him?" Mac said. "Or the train depot has cameras. Maybe we'll get lucky and catch him on tape."

"I'll do my best." Miss P's brow puckered. "You know, I lost another of my students that day. She had a heart attack. I believe she was traveling—"

The crash of breaking glass yanked their attention to the front of the room. Sam grabbed Miss P and pulled her under the table.

"Stay here." Mac commando crawled into her office and retrieved her pistol.

Standing inside her office doorway, she scanned the reception area. Her hand shook as she checked the magazine. A breeze stirred the curtain near the front door. She entered the room, gripping her gun with both hands and extending her arms in front of her.

Her heart slammed against her chest as she made her way forward. A rock sat on the floor amongst the shards of glass. She peered out the broken window. No one was in sight.

Thank you, Jesus.

Mac and Sam had taken defense classes with Sam's brother, Jake. He'd become a police officer while they'd started their private investigator firm. Mac prayed every day she'd never have to use her weapon. This was a good day.

"All clear." She stuck her gun in her waistband at her back and pulled on gloves she kept in a back pocket. "Someone sent us a message the old-fashioned way."

"What does it say?" Sam helped Miss P regain her seat.

Mac removed the paper tied to the rock.

"Wait." Miss P rose. "Do you have any large sandwich bags?"

"Good thinking." She placed the note in the clear bag. Three heads bent to read what it said.

STOP BOTHERING INNOCENT PEOPLE

"Good." Miss P slapped the table. "We must be on the right track."

Mac and Sam locked eyes. What had they gotten themselves into?

CHAPTER 3

"There's no we, Miss P," Mackenzie said. "This has taken a dangerous turn. We can't bring you into this."

"Nonsense." Miss P stiffened. "I can take care of myself. No small-minded idiot is going to scare me."

Miss P had been facing down classrooms of teenagers for more years than Mackenzie was alive. Mac and Sam could use her strength and positive attitude if nothing else.

"If I looked up backbone in the dictionary, your name would be there, Miss P." Mackenzie smiled at her.

"I'm taking that as a compliment," Miss Freebody's brow furrowed.

"It is."

"We should inform the police about this." Sam headed for her office. "I'm calling my brother."

Mac's stomach flipped. Jake was two years older than Mac. When she tried to analyze her reaction to him, she couldn't figure it out. He wasn't her usual type. But then, what was her type?

The first guy she'd been involved with was in college. A

long-haired, bearded hippie with a million-dollar name. Nathaniel Xander something. And the last guy she'd been attracted to turned out to be a thief nicknamed Prince Charming.

Jake Sanders wasn't a looker like Prince Charming, nor did he have a beard like Nate. His was a friendly face with a nose that had been broken when he was a kid. A genuine smile that he used a lot and showed teeth left to grow without the restriction of braces.

He wasn't a hunk like Samantha's husband, Alan, who worked as a personal trainer. Mac called *him* Macho Man.

But sometimes when Jake touched her ... there was just something about him. Jake possessed a natural assuredness. Not too full of himself and yet sure of his abilities. Women were drawn to him. But he remained single. Although she'd heard rumors about his dating life. She'd never had the guts to ask Sam if they were true.

Mac had thought about what it would be like to date Jake herself. But what if it didn't work out? He was Sam's brother, and she didn't want to jeopardize her relationship with her partner and friend. Mama always said, "Nothing is worth a broken relationship." Best to let that remain a dream. Besides, Jake never gave her any sign that he was interested in her at all, and she had no wish to become another of his trophies.

"Jake was already on his way. He's got something he wants to talk to us about." Sam walked over to the broken window. "We'll need to get this fixed after he sees it."

"We should take pictures ourselves." Miss Freebody pushed to her feet. "Shall I?"

"Be my guest."

A brisk knock sounded at the door before it opened. "Hello, you—" Detective Jake Sanders took off his hat. "Miss Freebody. I didn't know you were here."

"I forgot to mention that Miss P will be helping us on the case." Sam rushed over to greet her brother. "She's had forensics experience."

"I see." Jake cocked his head at his sister and mouthed, "Miss P?"

Sam nodded.

"Let's sit so I can get statements from all of you." Jake's eyes found Mackenzie's, a slight smile on his lips. He nodded his welcome. "We'll start with Mackenzie."

A lump formed in her throat, and she went in search of a glass of water.

JAKE FOCUSED on his notes as Mackenzie spoke. If he didn't, he wouldn't hear a word she said. He'd be too busy following the movement of her lips and wondering what they would feel like on his. It was getting more difficult to be around her. Harder to hide his attraction to her.

Mac had shown no interest in him, and the last thing he wanted was to cause trouble between her and his sister. What if he asked Mac on a date, and it didn't work out? Sam told him she'd been hurt once before. He didn't want to cause her additional pain. No. Best to leave it the way it was. Even if it meant he had to stop coming around and never see Mac again.

"Thanks." He glanced at his watch. "Let's break for lunch. I'll see if I can get some forensics guys in so you can get your window fixed."

"Detective, I could do the fingerprinting on the rock and the letter if you are amenable to that," Miss Freebody said. "I have kept up my certification and have a small lab in my home."

"Thank you for offering, but I'd have to run that by my chief first."

"Of course." She clasped her hands on the table and gave him an expectant look.

"Jake," Sam said. "I think she's waiting for you to make the call?"

"Gotcha." Jake pulled his cell from his pocket and walked into Sam's office. "Chief? I've got a situation here."

"What now?"

"Miss Freebody is here—"

"That woman is still breathing air?"

"Yes, sir, and she claims to be a certified forensics specialist." Jake glanced at the closed door between him and the women. "She wants to do the fingerprinting on the rock and the note."

"I believe she could do anything she put her mind to. Give her the okay. Besides, no use wasting the state's time and money on a prank."

"So, no forensics?"

"No."

"Thanks, Chief."

When he returned, a grin split his face. "It seems my chief knows you, Miss P. Lawrence Baker?"

"Yes, Lawrence. He was a good student. Although prone to daydreaming."

"He said he trusts you to do the fingerprinting on the rock and the note. He doesn't see the need to bother with forensics since someone threw the rock from the street, but I'll arrange to get your window patched until you can order a new one." Jake rubbed his hands together. "What do you ladies want from Sonic? My treat."

MAC DOVE into her meal like it was her last. She always ate when she was nervous—and being in the presence of Sam's brother made her very nervous. But, come to think of it, she ate when she was happy or sad—she just ate. How Mac stayed slim was one of God's many mysteries that she thanked Him for daily.

"What did you want to talk to us about?" Sam swallowed and glanced across the table at her brother.

"I almost forgot." Jake wiped his hands and left. When he returned, he laid a file on the table. "I'd like you two to look into a string of burglaries we've been having along the river."

"Burglaries?" Mac pushed her half-eaten sandwich away. "Why haven't we heard about them before?"

Jake glanced at her. Her hunger spiked, and she pulled her food toward her again.

"We worked hard to keep them quiet," he said. "We thought we'd get a quick arrest, but nothing so far. That's when I asked to bring you guys into it."

"How many have there been?" Sam pulled the file in front of her.

"Four so far. In four different cities, but all of them along the river."

"We're swamped trying to find—" Mac said.

"We'll look at it." Sam shot Mac *The Look.* "But I can't promise you anything, bro."

"That's all I ask." Jake smiled all around. "Ladies, it's been a pleasure. Duty calls."

Mac went in search of a cookie.

MACKENZIE STARED at her computer screen. Jake was gone, and she was stuffed. Miss P hurried home after lunch to begin work on the rock and the letter. All was quiet except for the clicking of Sam's nails on her keyboard.

A bang on the door brought Mac to her feet, heart pounding in her throat. She grabbed her revolver, held it at her side, and stood inside the closed door.

"Who is it?"

"Leonard Reese. I come to fix your window."

Mac pulled the door open. "I thought you were a mechanic."

"I do handyman stuff on the side." Reese scuffed his feet on the rug inside the door.

Mac suppressed a giggle as she remembered Miss P's comment about Leonard being good with his hands.

"I brought some plywood for now. You'll have to order a window."

"Thanks." Mac waved toward her office. "I'll be working."

Leonard's face paled. She forgot. She still held her revolver in her hand.

"Sorry. We're a little jumpy around here right now."

"Okay."

But he didn't sound okay. He sounded like a man who wanted to finish his job and get out of there.

"Hi, Leonard." Sam popped her head out of her office.

He gave her a weak smile and got to work, nailing the plywood into place with vigor.

Mac laid her revolver next to her computer and returned to her search. So many hotels in Kansas City. She'd started with those close to the train station and worked her way out in a circle. But no luck so far.

If Eleanor had checked in with someone else, Mac would never find it. Or if someone had picked her up and taken her to their home ... the options were endless. Mac could ask Connor if Eleanor had a friend in Kansas City. She wouldn't have to tell him why she was asking.

And she could use some exercise. She picked up her phone.

"Connor, it's Mackenzie Love. Are you free? Feel like a walk in Rennick Park?"

CHAPTER 4

The three flags at the plaza in James W. Rennick Riverfront Park cracked in the wind. Mackenzie snagged her jacket from the rear seat and walked to a nearby bench. She gazed at the tiers of rectangular brick buildings built on the ground sloping down to the river behind her.

Her German ancestors built Washington, Missouri, in an orderly fashion, with the main streets paralleling the Missouri River and side streets crisscrossing at right angles. Church steeples rose above the flat-topped roofs, pointing the way to heaven, and the train tracks followed the course of the river.

"Mackenzie?" Connor Davis came up beside her.

"Thanks for meeting me." Mackenzie pulled her light jacket closer. "You'd think after growing up here I'd remember how cool the breeze can be coming off the river. But it always surprises me."

They strolled around the old water works building until they came to a bench facing the Missouri River.

"The river is one reason Eleanor and I moved back." Connor gazed at the white caps forming on its surface.

"I'm so sorry for all you've been through." Mac laid a hand on his arm. "First being accused of killing your wife and then, after being proven innocent ..." She glanced over her shoulder toward town.

"I don't blame them." He stuffed his hands in his pockets. "Who didn't love Eleanor? I was the kid from the wrong side of the tracks who married the boss's daughter." He pinched the bridge of his nose. "I miss her so much."

Mac's heart lurched in her chest.

"I wanted to ask you a question," she said. "Maybe this is a bad time."

"No. It's fine." He pulled a milk chocolate bar from his pocket. "I'm trying to quit smoking. But, unfortunately, now I'm addicted to these. Want some?"

"No thanks. I'm a dark chocolate person." Mac drew her jacket closer. "As you know, I'm working to find out who kil— did this to Eleanor." Connor's expression became guarded. "Do you know if Eleanor had any friends in Kansas City?"

He lifted his gaze in thought. "No, I don't believe so." The dark shadow of a frown transformed his face. "Why?"

"I'd heard she made frequent trips there by train. Just wondered why."

His posture loosened. Had he expected her to say something else?

"To shop." Connor gave her a sad smile. "She loved the clothes at a couple of stores there."

"That explains it." But there'd been no new items in her suitcase the day she was killed.

"Mackenzie," Connor stood. "I don't know how to say this after all you've done for me, but please stop this investigation." Tears flowed freely down his cheeks. "It's too painful."

"Don't you want to know who killed her?" Mac got to her feet.

"No. I need to move on with my life." Connor placed a hand over his heart. "I'll pay you for any time you've spent."

"That's not necessary." She gave him a small smile. "I'll ... think about it."

"Good. And thank you again." He threw his chocolate wrapper in the trashcan and walked away.

Unease crawled up Mac's spine. What was Connor afraid of? Even if Eleanor was about to divorce him, he'd already been acquitted of her murder. So why had he asked her to back off?

Mackenzie steered her car left out of the parking lot onto Lafayette St. A bell clanged, and red lights flashed as a red and white arm lowered across the road. She groaned. With the customary blasts of its whistle, two longs, a short, and a long, an orange engine pulling a freight train barreled past her. Its wash rocked her four-door sedan as she waited to cross.

Eleanor's trip to Kansas City had something to do with her death. And Connor did not want her to investigate it. Could he have thrown the rock through her window? He didn't seem the type.

The last boxcar sped past, and the arm raised. Mac put her car in gear and bumped over the tracks. With at least two people trying to stop her investigation, she couldn't help but wonder what they were afraid she'd find? Next stop, the train station.

"Good afternoon." Mac flashed her credentials in front of the lady in the gift shop. "I wonder if you could help me."

"Possibly. What do you want?"

"I'd like to see your security footage for April."

"Why?"

Mac paused. "It's for a case I'm working."

"Aren't you the one who got Connor Davis off for killing his wife?" The woman peered at her.

25

"I found the man he had lunch with, yes." Was this how the townspeople would remember her for the rest of her life?

"Do you have a warrant?"

"No." Heat rose along Mac's neck to her face. "I thought you might be interested in helping find who really killed Mrs. Davis."

"We know who killed her." The woman glared at her. "But he got away with it. So, unless you have a warrant, we have nothing more to talk about."

Mac forced her face into a smile and left. Once outside, she struggled to contain a scream of frustration and anger. Praying she wouldn't encounter another irate citizen of her hometown, she hurried to her car. She'd had enough for one day.

Maybe she should drop the investigation, wait until things died down, and begin again. She hadn't expected all this hatred. It hurt more than she let on. Mama's voice sounded in Mac's head. "Whatever you do in life, Mackenzie, remember who you're really working for. The opinion of men doesn't matter if you're following the path God set before you." Sadness pushed on Mac's shoulders, weighing her down. She didn't have the faith that mama had. How would she know if she was doing what God intended?

All she knew for sure was that she wasn't ready to give up yet. She pulled her cellphone from her purse, dialed, and waited, heart pulsing in her throat.

"Detective Sanders—Jake?" Mackenzie cleared her throat. "I have a favor to ask."

"Hi, Mackenzie. Be glad to help if I can."

"I'm at the train station and a lead ... it's a long story. Anyway, I'd like to look at some surveillance video, but the woman in charge insists on a warrant." Mackenzie paused. "Can you get me one?"

"Not me, but the Chief can. I'll need more details. Why don't you come by the station?"

"Okay." Mackenzie hung up.

Her stomach butterflied. Two visits with Jake in one day. Hey, she'd initiated this one—she needed the warrant to move forward. She started her car and aimed for the police station.

"Mama, if you can hear me, I could use some of your direction about now."

A billboard caught Mac's eye advertising a popular soft drink. "Life is short. Live it with gusto."

Mackenzie laughed. "Got it."

After a few turns, Mac pulled into the parking lot in front of the Public Safety Building. Jake stood in front of the glass doors and motioned for her to stop.

She rolled her window down. "That was quick. Your boss is—"

"I'm sorry, Mac." Jake squatted next to her car. "The Chief wouldn't get you a warrant."

"But he hasn't heard my reasons yet."

"I know." Jake held up a hand. "But ..."

"But what?" Mac bit her lip to keep from yelling, but her sarcasm was clear.

"Nothing." He shook his head and stepped away from her car. "I'm sorry."

As her window closed, Jake spoke again. "You know, the old Meerschaum pipe factory has had a lot of vandalism lately."

She flung the car door open. Then, after a moment of struggling with the seatbelt, she stood toe-to-toe with Jake. Not quite the effect she'd hoped for, but close. "Are you telling me that if I agree to investigate this vandalism, the Chief will get me my warrant? You scratch my back, I'll scratch yours?"

"No, Mac." Jake held his hand up. "I was giving you a hint

about where to go next. Think about it." He dropped his hand and moved around her. "I need to get to work. I'll call later."

She lowered herself into the driver's seat. What did mischief at the pipe factory have to do with her case? She drove slowly through the narrow streets of downtown Washington until she was in front of the old Missouri Meerschaum factory. The plan was to turn it into studio apartments and luxury condos.

Mac pulled to the curb and got out. The windows on this side of the building would have an unobstructed view of the river. The only thing between them and the water was the parking lot for the ... train.

She spun around and scanned the building. A small smile lifted the corners of her mouth. That was what Jake meant. Two cameras hung from the brick façade under the eaves, and they both pointed toward the street and parking lot beyond.

But did the security company still have video from April, and more importantly, would she be allowed to view it?

CHAPTER 5

J ake stood inside the glass entry doors to the Public Safety Building and watched Mackenzie drive away. Her scent of peppermint and something else he didn't recognize lingered in his memory. He longed to go after her—to tell her he'd help her and that he ... what? Cared about her? More? He took his hand off the door handle. Not a good idea. Somehow, he knew he would be of more use to her here.

When he entered the squad room, Chief Baker was waiting for him. "I saw you and Mackenzie through the window. She didn't look happy."

"No, sir." Jake kept his gaze averted and headed for his desk.

"I have my reasons, Detective." Chief Baker put an arm out, blocking Jake's way. "Remember who you work for."

"Yes, sir."

Baker dropped his arm, and Jake continued on his way. He wished his boss would explain why he got so upset when Jake asked about a warrant for Mac. At least tell him something he could pass on to her that made sense.

Jake opened his computer and scrolled through recent crimes in the area. Pretty quiet, except for the burglaries. The latest one happened in Jefferson City with the same modus operandi. The owners were out of town, no alarm on the house, and only something easily transported but extremely valuable taken.

Wonder if Mac and Sam had had a chance to study the file yet? Maybe he should check and take them this latest information. The heaviness in his chest lifted a little.

A BELL SOUNDED as Mac entered the small shop and museum on the corner of the pipe factory building.

"May I help you?" A man sat behind a counter in the shadows to her right.

"I hope so." Mac squinted at him. "I know you. We were in Sunday school together."

He stood. "And you're a private investigator now. You've really stirred things up around here lately."

"Yes." Her hopes of seeing the security tapes vanished like the Cheshire cat in Alice in Wonderland. Still … "I was wondering if you could help me."

He polished his glasses on his shirttail. "That depends on what you need."

"I noticed you have cameras on the outside of the building. Would I be able to view your security footage from last April?"

"That was six months ago." He gave her a sideways look. "Most security cameras only keep footage for a month, but …"

She fought to tamp down the scream forming in her throat. *Get on with it, please.*

"… because we've been having trouble, the owner is super conservative and insists we save every frame in case we need it for a trial." He rolled his eyes. "What are you interested in seeing?" He led the way to a locked door in the rear of the museum.

"Two days in April." Mac gave him the dates and silently blessed his boss for being cautious.

"Okay." He sat in front of a bank of monitors and selected a tape from a stack of six or seven, each labeled with a different month.

He inserted the tape, pressed a few keys, and an image appeared on the central screen. After several minutes of fast-forwarding, he stopped on a black and white view of the street in front of the building and the parking lot beyond. Mac leaned closer. Leonard Reese worked under the hood of an older model Lexus.

As the minutes passed, another car entered the parking lot. Eleanor Davis got out of the driver's seat, and a man in a hat and coat exited the passenger's door. They retrieved their luggage. She locked the car, and they walked toward the station.

Leonard slammed the hood on the Lexus, wiped his hands on a rag, and trailed after them. Just like he'd said. The man on the screen kept his face covered, and it was too far to see his pinky finger. At least it proved Leonard Reese was telling the truth.

"Is there any way I could get a copy of that?" She straightened.

"I guess so." The man at the console shifted in his chair. "I shouldn't be showing you these, but I feel sorry for you. I know what it's like to be on the bad side of people."

"Thanks." Mac searched her memory for what she knew about the man helping her, but all she remembered was being in church school with him. "I'll need a copy of the Saturday tape as well." Probably nothing useful on that one, either. But at least it might show Eleanor returned on the train on the day of her death and wasn't leaving like the police initially thought.

Before leaving the store, she turned. "Thanks again for the help. If there's ever anything I can do for you, look me up."

"I might take you up on that one day."

Mac walked toward her car. What a nice guy, and she almost went off on him for no reason.

She knew what Mama would say. "You control your emotions, or you allow your emotions to control you." But it wasn't easy with a murder to solve and a spate of burglaries to investigate. She touched her purse. The first real breakthrough might be on these memory sticks.

A piece of paper fluttered in the breeze under her windshield wiper. Did she get a ticket? For what? She yanked it out, annoyance rising like bile in her throat. But it wasn't a ticket.

THIS IS YOUR SECOND WARNING! STOP! WE ALREADY KNOW WHO THE MURDERER IS!

Mackenzie's stomach knotted as she fumbled with her car door handle. Was he following her? Watching her right now? Once inside, she pressed the door lock button and willed her hands to stop shaking. She placed the note in a baggie for examination later—not that she expected to find anything of consequence.

A frisson of fear traveled through her. Was this the killer or someone out for revenge because she helped Connor? She started her car and pulled away from the curb, anxious to return to her office.

As she pulled into the narrow driveway next to the office, a large sedan turned the corner and parked out front. Mackenzie grabbed her phone and pressed the number on speed dial for Samantha.

"What's up, my friend?"

"I'm outside and—never mind." Mac punched End as Miss Freebody emerged from the driver's door. She leaned her head back and closed her eyes.

"Mackenzie?" Miss P peered in her window. "Are you quite all right, my dear?"

She managed a nod and a weak smile. "Let's go in, and I'll explain."

"What's going on?" Samantha met them. Her heart-shaped face creased with concern.

"I'm not sure." Miss P held the door for Mac. "I discovered Mackenzie sitting outside as if she'd had a fright."

"I could use a tall glass of iced tea." Mac pulled out a chair at the table in the center of the room. "With lots of sugar."

"I'll pour one for each of us." Miss Freebody headed for the kitchen.

Sam raised an eyebrow at her partner, but Mac shook her head. She only wanted to go through her story once.

Miss P returned. "Three tall glasses of very sweet tea."

Mac grasped hers and took a long drink. Better.

"I found security footage of Eleanor arriving at the train station on Thursday, and hopefully, again on Saturday." Mac deposited the thumb drives on the table. "I haven't seen the Saturday one yet."

"Where did you get these?" Sam picked them up and stepped into her office.

Mac and Miss P followed.

"The pipe factory has cameras trained in that direction. I asked, and the guy gave them to me." Mac gave them a brief smile. "He knew me from Sunday school a long time ago, and he said he felt sorry for me. Whatever the reason, I count it as a miracle considering the attitude of most in the town."

"Not everyone feels the same, Mackenzie, I can assure you." Miss P patted her shoulder.

"Well, at least one person is feeling threatened by my—our investigation." Mac withdrew the note from her windshield and handed it to Miss P. "Would you see if you can find any prints on this?"

"I will." Miss P's face hardened as she read the message. "I couldn't raise any prints from the rock or the other note. Hopefully, this one will yield better results."

"Did you call Jake?" Sam looked up from her computer.

"No." Mac stiffened. How could she tell her friend that Jake wanted nothing to do with their investigation—and she wanted nothing to do with him—without causing a rift between brother and sister or a chasm between her and her friend?

"We need to." Sam reached for her phone.

"Don't." Mac placed a hand on her partner's. "It might cause trouble for your brother. I think he finds himself caught between his boss and his sister—and her friend. We need to leave him out of this."

"Why do you say that?" Sam chewed on her bottom lip. "Chief Baker is a reasonable man. He'd never give Jake grief—"

"I asked Jake for a warrant to see the security footage at the train station, and the Chief denied it without even listening to my reasons. Jake agreed with him." No longer able to contain the mix of emotions seething inside, Mac hurried from the room.

The front door opened, and Detective Jake Sanders stepped in. "Hello, ladies. Thought I'd—"

Mackenzie charged past him into her office and slammed the door.

CHAPTER 6

J ake's throat closed around his words, and he stared at the
door to his left. Coming here was a bad idea.

"It's okay, Jake." Samantha linked her arm through
his. "Mac needs a break. What brings you here?"

Sam led him to the table in the center of the room. Miss P
gathered some of the papers covering the surface into piles and
made room for him to sit.

"Would you like some tea or coffee, Detective?" Miss
Freebody said.

"Coffee, thanks." He glanced over his shoulder at Mac's
office door before taking a seat. His churning gut told him
there was more to her retreat than Sam let on. "What actually
happened?"

"She was upset because your chief wouldn't help her." Sam
sighed. "And she believes you agreed with him."

"I didn't, but he's my boss. What was I supposed to do?"
Jake leaned toward her. "I tried to help—I told her about the
pipe factory cameras."

Sam raised a hand, palm out. "I understand. And she will,

too, once she's had time to calm down. Right now, her feelings are bruised. Practically the whole town acts like she's the enemy, and she's sensitive to anything that smells like a slight."

He ached to barge into her office, take her in his arms—

"Don't even think about it," Sam said.

How did she do that? His sister had always been able to read his thoughts.

"Now." She patted his arm. "Why have you graced us with your presence?"

Miss P set a mug in front of him.

"Thanks." He took a sip, his mind whirling with images of the woman in the other room. Why had he come? He glimpsed the folder before him.

"I wanted to see if you'd looked at the burglary file." He slid a file across the table. "And to bring you the latest case."

"I've studied the file, Detective." Miss P scanned some notes in front of her. "But I haven't discerned any pattern yet. Where and when did this latest burglary take place?"

"Jeff City at around eleven in the morning. Three days ago."

"Hmm." Miss P extracted a map from a pile of papers. "Something about these burglaries and their timing niggles at me."

"Keep at it, Miss P. If anyone can crack this case, you can."

"You're too kind."

"I need to get back to work." Jake stood, but his eyes strayed to Mac's door. "Maybe I ..."

"No." Sam took his arm and walked him to the front door. "Not today, Jake." She gave him a quick hug. "Good to see you. We'll let you know if we come up with any ideas about the thefts."

He said goodbye and crossed the lawn to his patrol car. A dull pain settled between his eyes, and he rubbed his forehead.

He sure hoped Sam was right and Mac would understand because the thought of losing his friendship with Mac left a hollow pit in his stomach.

MAC JOINED her friends in the main room. "I'm sorry you guys had to see me wreck on the rocks like that."

"Hey, what are friends for?" Sam gave her shoulders a quick hug.

"Certainly, my dear. You've had to deal with a lot today, but I assure you, it will get better." Miss P smiled at her across the table.

"Thanks." The warmth of their friendship eased the ache in her heart. But what about Jake? How could things ever get better with him?

"Let's look at the pipe store security footage from Saturday, the day Eleanor was killed."

The women gathered around Sam's computer screen and watched as the train arrived. Five minutes later, Eleanor Davis appeared with a bag over her shoulder, dragging one behind her.

"There she is." Sam nodded at the image on the screen.

Another couple came into view as Eleanor lifted her luggage into her trunk. They got into a dark blue SUV parked across and down from Eleanor.

"It seems they may have been the only people on the train that day."

"There could have been more," Mac said. "There're a few parking spots by the station we can't see from here."

Eleanor waited for a car to pass before making a left out of the parking lot. A motorcycle and a truck came behind her. When the SUV turned, it crossed in front of a bus.

The women gasped.

"That was close," Mac said. Why risk an accident with a bus to gain a few more minutes or a place in traffic?

No other vehicles were in the train parking lot or on the street.

"At least now we know for sure she took the train back from Kansas City on Saturday." Sam stopped the video.

"And pinky finger man didn't return with her."

Mac led the way out of Sam's office. She turned her back on the conference table covered in manilla folders, newspaper clippings, and note cards and plopped into a chair in the reception area. How long had it been since she'd eaten anything? Sonic with Sam, Miss P, and ... Jake. She'd rest her eyes a moment and then grab a sandwich.

"I made soup. Let me straighten my papers and heat some for us."

"Bless you, Miss P," Sam said.

Soon the aroma of vegetables and spices in a tomato broth wafted through the air, rousing Mac from her stupor. *Yes, bless you, Miss P.*

"Time to rock and roll, girlfriend." Sam held out a hand to help Mac up. "We need to decide where we go from here."

Mac took her friend's hand and stood. Sam's steady gaze held hers. Time to rock and roll. She squeezed Sam's hand and walked over to the table. "Smells delicious, Miss P."

"I made plenty." She placed two bowls in front of the women. "You two need more vegetables." The older woman sat and bowed her head. "For this food which we are about to receive, may we be truly thankful. Amen."

"Amen."

"Amen."

Mac and Sam were in perfect sync, a testament to their long friendship.

"Let's discuss our next move." Mac reached for some crackers nearby. "I think we still need to find out who the man is who got on the train with her before she died. Even if he didn't kill her, he might know something important." Mac glanced at the other two women, who nodded in agreement.

"I will look for a print on the second note, although it occurs to me that whoever put it on your car should be on video."

"You're right." Mac thumped her forehead with the ball of her hand. "I should have thought of that."

"And I'll continue studying the files on the burglaries while you and Samantha investigate any leads elsewhere." A deep crease formed on Miss P's brow. "There's a pattern to these crimes. I know it's there, but my poor old brain isn't what it used to be. It's very frustrating."

Sam laid a hand on the older woman's arm. "You're sharper than Mac and I combined. You'll get it worked out."

"Thank you for that vote of confidence, my dear." Miss P moved her bowl aside. "What do you two intend to do now?"

Mac swallowed a spoonful of soup. "I told my sister I'd come see her this weekend. I leave for Kansas City in two days, but I'm taking the train instead of driving. Maybe I can find the conductor who saw Eleanor and pinky finger boarding that Thursday." She barked a laugh. "My chances are as good as finding a white cat in a blizzard, but you never know."

"I'll try to find—no—I'll find out where she stayed—and before you leave Kansas City, you can discover the clue that breaks the case wide open." Sam grinned. "How's that for positive?"

"In the meantime—" Mac chuckled. "—we'll look at the security footage again, go back over the file one more time, and I'll return to the museum to see who left the note under my wiper."

Sam glanced at her watch. "Need to run. Thanks again for the soup, Miss P. See you tomorrow."

"We should all head for home and get some sleep." Mac rose. "We can take care of the dishes tomorrow, Miss P."

"They won't take long, Mackenzie." Miss P gathered the bowls and walked to the kitchen.

"Sam, go on." Mac stood. "I'll help wash up."

Half an hour later, Mac dried the last bowl, and the women prepared to leave. Puddles on the pavement and sidewalk reflected the glow of the streetlamps in the gathering darkness. Mac double-checked the alarm and locked the door.

She studied the exterior of their building while waiting for Miss P to leave. It would need a new roof within the next year. She sighed. They'd worry about that when the time came.

The top floor of the office once held two additional bedrooms, currently used for storage. One room contained a cot in case one of them felt the need to rest for a minute.

Once, Mac thought about living above their offices but decided against it. Too much trouble. She'd have to get someone in to fix up the place. Besides, she liked having a separate space where she could get away from work.

She bought her parents' house from their estate after they passed away. Every evening, she navigated the familiar route from the office to her childhood home, her mind free to mull over the day's events.

As she started for home, a pair of headlights swung in behind her.

CHAPTER 7

At 5th Street, Mac turned right. The headlights behind her turned right. When she sped up, they sped up, and when she slowed, they slowed. Mac fumbled with her phone.

"Jake, is that you behind me?"

"What are you talking about?"

"If it's not you, then somebody's following me."

"Where are you?"

"I'm pulling into my driveway."

"Stay inside your car with the doors locked. I'm on my way."

Mac swung into her driveway, jerked her seatbelt off, and twisted around to peer through her rear window. Her heart pounded in her throat. No car passed by. Two minutes later, Jake's patrol car screamed up, sirens and lights blaring. She got out and leaned on her door.

"Are you all right?"

"Yes." The adrenaline release left her shaking.

"What kind of car was it?"

"I only glimpsed it. Maybe a van? Dark blue or black? When

I pulled in, I waited, but it never came past me." Mac bit her lip. "Maybe I'm imagining things."

"I don't think so." Jake studied her. "Let's get you inside." He retrieved her purse and phone. "When this happens again, call me and drive to the police station."

When this happens again? "You believe me." Her eyes searched his for reassurance. "I was being followed."

"Yes." Jake's tone was grim. "Whoever's threatening you will not stop unless you quit searching for who killed Eleanor Davis. Knowing you, I can't see that happening."

AFTER MAKING sure Mac locked her door behind him, Jake steered his car toward police headquarters. He took the stairs two at a time and rapped on the Chief's open door. "We need to talk."

"Come in." Baker closed the file he was reading and leaned back in his chair. "What's on your mind?"

"Somebody tailed Mac home tonight." Jake rubbed the back of his neck. "She thought it was me, but I was in another neighborhood."

Chief Baker sat up and put his elbows on his desk. "You're sure?"

"Mac doesn't imagine things."

"What do you want from me?"

Jake blew out a breath. He knew what he wanted to ask, but did he dare? Would he lose his job?

"Out with it, Sanders. I haven't got all night."

"Sir, do you feel like the rest of the town—that Mac and Sam helped get a killer off and that they have no right investigating the Eleanor Davis murder?"

Chief Baker's face turned to stone. "This is about the

warrant this morning." He folded his hands. "I knew Davis didn't kill his wife, but I also knew whoever did wouldn't like her messing with the case. And I was right. I was trying to discourage her. This is a police matter."

"She doesn't discourage easily. Neither does my sister."

"I can see that." The Chief narrowed his eyes at Jake. "I'm giving you two assignments. Investigate the threats and get those two to drop the case. Distract them. Get them interested in those burglaries. Do whatever you have to. Only keep them safe. I won't have another murder in my town." The Chief opened the file on his desk and picked up his pen. "Keep me posted."

"Yes, sir." *The Chief must think I'm a miracle worker.* A weight settled in his stomach.

Jake took the stairs to the first floor and swiped his card to leave the building. A breeze dried the sweat on his skin. He leaned against his car and crossed his arms. With its cool temperatures and harvest moons, Autumn was his favorite time of year, but its charms failed to soothe his soul tonight.

"Dad, I wish you were here. I could sure use some of your wisdom about now." He pulled his phone from his pocket.

Eight o'clock. Too late to call his parents in Florida. They'd be in bed. Besides, his father didn't always recognize him nowadays. But he owed mom a call. Tomorrow.

His stomach growled as he started his car. A stop at Cowans before going home sounded good.

"Honey, I'm home." Jake stepped inside his little house and rattled the bag of food.

In the kitchen, the aromas of a hamburger with onions and French fries filled the small space. Jake pulled a paper plate from the cupboard and dumped the fries on it.

"The server put something special in here for you too." He looked around.

A sleek gray cat with black stripes strolled into the room and sat on the mat by Jake's feet.

"No date tonight?" He bent to stroke the cat's back. A glance at the small opening set into the back door told the story. "Oops. I forgot to unlock your cat door this morning. Sorry." He shook the chicken pieces into a bowl and placed them before the animal. "Hope this makes up for my mistake."

"*Mwarw.*" The regal cat rubbed his head against Jake's hand and began to eat.

Jake took his food to the table. "I'm glad you're here, Duke. I need a good listener."

Duke turned brilliant green eyes on Jake briefly before returning to his dinner.

"We've talked about how I feel about Mac." Jake sipped his drink. "But now she thinks I'm siding with the Chief and the Chief is siding with the town. None of which is true. What do I do?"

Duke jumped into Jake's lap and nuzzled his chest.

Jake laughed. "I don't think she'd let me do that. In fact, I'm sure I'd be a dead man. Any other suggestions?"

Duke leaped down and returned with a piece of chicken, which he deposited on Jake's plate.

Jake stared. "Duke, sometimes you scare me." He stroked his cat's back.

CHAPTER 8

A fter a fitful sleep filled with dreams of being chased, Mac gave up. She climbed out of bed, dressed, and left for work. But she still didn't beat Miss P.

The aroma of frying eggs, bacon, and coffee greeted her as she opened the door. "Am I in time for breakfast?"

"Certainly, my dear." Miss P bustled out of the kitchen with a plate and set it before her. "I'll get mine and join you."

Mac gathered silverware and napkins. How had Miss P known she'd be there?

"Knock, knock. Do I smell bacon?" Jake took a step inside.

"Sit down, young man. I'll bring you a plate."

"I can help with coffee." He sat a bag by Mac's plate.

"You're here early." Mac forked a piece of egg. "What's in the bag?"

"A little something for you." Jake eyed Mac over the rim of his mug. "And I want to give you a message from the Chief."

He'd brought her a present. Mac tried to ignore the tingling in her body. "And I want to know how you, Miss P, knew to expect us so early this morning."

"I heard the call on my scanner last evening." Miss P took a sip of coffee. "I came in and made breakfast on the off chance you might show up."

"You're amazing." Mac smiled at her. She slid Jake a curious look. "What's the message from your boss?"

"He's never believed that Connor Davis killed his wife. The only reason he wants you to stop investigating the Davis murder is that he's concerned about your safety." Jake sat his mug on the table. "In fact, he put me in charge of finding out who's behind the threats and keeping you and Sam safe."

"So that's why you responded so fast last night."

"Not the only reason." His deep blue eyes blazed with a look she couldn't decipher. "But right now, we need to focus on what's next."

Mac pulled her plate closer and picked up a piece of bacon. "My sisters want me to come visit them in Kansas City for a couple of days. Maybe that would be a good idea."

"Great. Why don't you open your bag?" Jake nodded.

Mac undid the ribbon and pulled out a beautiful blue patterned scarf. "Jake, it's gorgeous. But why? It's not my birthday."

"An apology for yesterday." He smiled at her. "You can wear it to Kansas City. I'll give you a ride."

"I think I'll take the train. It's relaxing, and maybe I can find the conductor who saw Eleanor and pinky finger man together."

"Eleanor and pinky finger man?"

"That's right. You don't know." Mac stopped mid-bite. "We have a source who saw Eleanor and a man get on the train the Thursday before she died."

"Why didn't you tell me this?"

"You didn't give me a chance. Remember?"

He remembered. If he'd listened to her ... if he'd made his chief listen to her ...

"Anyway, the man has half his pinky finger on his left hand missing."

"Okay." Jake made a note on his phone. "I'll see what I can find on a man with a missing pinky finger."

"I will continue to work on the burglaries," Miss Freebody said. "I believe I'm close to a breakthrough."

Mac had forgotten about the burglaries. "Maybe Sam can help you with those while I'm gone."

"By the way, I was able to lift a partial fingerprint from the second threatening note."

"What second note?" Jake's voice took on a hard edge.

"Somebody put it on my windshield when I came out of the pipe factory. Miss P will make you a copy. Wait." She lifted a hand off the table. "I never got back to see if their cameras caught the guy on tape. Miss P, can you do that?" What else did Jake need to know? "The pipe factory cameras show Eleanor returned on the Saturday train and—"

"You mean she returned on the train the day she was killed?" Jake pushed his plate into the middle of the table. "She wasn't leaving? What else haven't you told me?"

Mac gave him a sheepish smile. "I think that's it."

"I'll check with the museum about the day you were there, and I need to see the footage you brought back," Jake said.

"It's in Sam's office." Mac pushed up from the table. "We can look at it now. I don't catch the train until five."

Jake motioned for her to sit. "Later. Let's wait for Sam." He stood and peered out the front window. "Stay here. I need to make a call." He shrugged into his jacket and stepped outside.

"I'm going to need some help, Chief." Jake paced along the sidewalk outside the office.

"What kind of help?"

"It's more complicated than we thought." Jake told his boss all he'd learned from Mac at breakfast. "I need someone to search the database for a man with a missing pinky finger. I need access to railroad security footage and their passenger records. And I need a fingerprint from another note run through the system. Also, I'll need camera footage checked at the pipe museum."

"I told you to investigate the threats, Sanders, and to stop them looking into the Davis murder, not to help them."

Jake turned his back on the house. Could they hear the Chief's booming voice? "Yes, sir, but I know these two. They won't stop. The only way I'll—we'll—be able to keep them safe is to help them." He gripped the phone tighter as if he could hold off the storm of frustration and anger he knew was happening on the other end.

"You can have Detective Victor Young. But Sanders, if so much as a hair is hurt on either of these two women, you will be in a patrol car the rest of your life. Got it?" The Chief's voice was low and his speech slow. He meant every word.

"Got it." A chill raced through Jake. The lives of two of the women he cared about most in the world rested in his hands. Was he up to the task? He muttered a prayer and walked inside.

Mac called to him from her office. "I'm going home to get ready for my trip and take a nap." She yawned. "Or maybe the other way around." She gathered some papers together and put them in a tote.

"I'll follow you and then go back to the station. I've got work to do."

"You don't have to babysit me. I can take care of myself."

He raised an eyebrow at her, and she blushed.

"Last night I got scared. I wasn't prepared, but I am now."

"That's what I'm afraid of." Jake's stomach clenched.

REFRESHED AND SHOWERED, Mac looked forward to the visit with her sisters—make that sister. Beth had a work trip, but Kate was in town. Maybe she could forget about threatening notes and murder for a few days. The doorbell rang. Her ride to the train had arrived.

Mac pulled her rolling overnight case across the living room. "I think I've got everything. What I don't have, Kate will. Except for my phone. Got to have my phone. My ticket's on that."

"Right here." Jake held it out to her. "I wouldn't let you get out of here without that."

She reached for her phone, but he held on to it. She looked at him. "What?"

He stepped closer, his dark blue eyes filled with an emotion she wasn't ready to acknowledge. "Mac, I ... Promise me you'll be careful."

"I promise." She pulled her phone from his grasp, her heart beating hard in her chest. "Although I don't plan on doing anything more dangerous than trying on clothes." She gave a shaky laugh.

"Good." He pulled her suitcase to the trunk of his cruiser and escorted her to the front seat.

As he got behind the steering wheel, she glanced at him. "Thanks for the ride and the present." She touched the scarf around her neck.

"My pleasure." Jake kept his eyes straight ahead.

Had she imagined the look in his eyes?

At the train station, Mac followed Jake to the boarding area. Should she shake his hand? Hug him? She settled for a brief smile. "A visit with my sisters will be good for me, and by the time I return, things will have calmed down." She showed her ticket on her phone to the conductor and boarded the train. "I don't want to cause any more trouble for you with your boss."

"I told you he's okay with it." He handed her the roller bag. "Be careful."

"I will." She opened her mouth to say more, but the conductor swung onto the train between her and Jake.

The engineer blew the warning whistle, and the train glided forward as she settled into her seat. She closed her eyes and let the tensions of the last few days ease away with each mile.

At least she tried to. Half an hour into her journey, they pulled into the Hermann, Missouri, station.

The train from Kansas City would have stopped in Hermann on the day Eleanor Davis was killed. At the time, her husband was meeting his friend in this same town for lunch. Less than an hour later, she was dead. Who else wanted Eleanor dead?

After five more stops and four hours, the train left the farms and small towns for pavement and a forest of tall buildings. Day had turned to night, but lights blazed in many of the skyscrapers. Mac glanced at her watch. Were there people still working? Or maybe those were apartment buildings?

She followed her fellow passengers into Kansas City Union Station and stopped as she caught sight of the 95-foot ceiling of the Grand Hall. It always took her breath away. The three massive chandeliers threw a golden glow on the space. Sounds of life echoed off marble and granite walls, and the smells from vendors made her stomach growl. When had she eaten last?

She texted her sister, Kate.

where r u?

b right there

Mac headed for the door. On second thought, she'd get a candy bar. She pivoted and collided with a man behind her. "Sorry. Are you okay?"

The man grabbed her arm to keep her from falling. "My fault." He smiled at her and hurried on.

Mac watched the man go. The hairs on the back of her neck stood up. There was something about him, but her brain was on strike. As Daddy used to say, her "get up and go had got up and went."

She paid for her candy bar and went out into the cool October night to meet her sister.

As Jake watched Mac's train pull away, his phone rang. "Hi, Sam."

"Why don't you have dinner with Alan and me tonight? It's fried chicken night."

His first reaction was to say no. His sister and her husband had so little time together, and he hated to intrude. But tonight, he could use the company.

"Sure. Want me to bring anything?" He took the walkway to the parking lot.

"Just yourself."

What was it about his sister? She always seemed to know

when he needed a lift. She was a lot like Mom. Which reminded him, he owed her a call. He hit a number on speed dial.

"Jake, I was just thinking about you."

His mother's voice brought a smile to his face. "Same here."

"Well, you know what they say about great minds."

He laughed. "At least one great mind. I can't vouch for the other one." He leaned against his car.

"Jake Sanders, not a nice thing to say about your mother." Her chuckle sounded like she stood right next to him. "How are things in Washington? I hear your sister and Mac have managed to turn things upside down."

"As usual." He ran a hand through his hair. "The Chief finally agreed that we need to help them."

"I'm glad to hear that. I was worried."

He heard a voice in the background.

"I need to go. Your dad needs my help. We'll talk soon."

"Love you, Mom." Jake swallowed the sadness in his throat. "Tell Dad I love him too."

"I love you, too, son, and so does your dad."

The line went dead.

Jake started his car and drove to his sister's house.

"You've been talking to Mom." Sam stared at him.

How did she know this stuff?

"I can always tell when you get that sad look." She linked her arm through his. "Come eat and you'll feel better."

"I keep thinking I should move to Florida. Help Mom out with Dad."

Sam turned Jake to face her. "The only joy Mom has is that you and I are doing what we love. If you move there, you'll be stealing a big part of her joy."

"How can you be so sure?"

"Because she and I had this discussion several months ago.

When Dad's dementia first started." Tears flooded her eyes. "She assured me that if she felt in need of help, she'd let us know. We have to respect her judgment."

He nodded. His sister continued to amaze him, and he thanked God for her every day.

JAKE ARRIVED home content in stomach and soul. But his mind still churned with all he'd learned today. No wonder Mac was being threatened. She and Sam were making genuine progress on the case. More than the police had. At least Mac was safe in Kansas City for now, and Sam had Alan to watch over her. Nobody would mess with him.

He should get some sleep. Tomorrow would be a long day. He laid down and closed his eyes, but his mind refused to shut off. Who was the man with the mutilated finger? Why hadn't the police realized Eleanor had returned on the train the day she died?

And why was he such an idiot? He went over the scene at Mac's house again. It was obvious she didn't feel the same about him as he did for her.

He rolled onto his side and yanked the quilt over his shoulders.

"*Mrawr.*" Duke jumped on the bed next to him.

"Finally decided to come see me, huh?" He scratched under his chin. "Where you been? Never mind. I don't want to know."

After kneading the covers some, the cat curled into a ball against Jake's chest. Soon, both were fast asleep.

CHAPTER 9

J ake woke to the ringing of his phone. He tracked the annoying sound to his jacket in the living room where he'd left it. "What?"

"Excuse me, Detective, did I wake you?"

Jake groaned under his breath. "Sorry, Miss P."

"It's quite all right, young man. I was wondering if you intended to join your sister and myself at the office today."

"Yes, ma'am." Jake peered at the time. Seven-thirty. Since when did sis get to work so early? "Is Sam there?"

"She's on her way."

"I'll be there in a half-hour." Shower. He ran his fingers over his face. Shave. And a cup of coffee. Coffee first.

"Mrawr." Duke rubbed against his legs.

Jake picked the handsome animal up and carried him into the kitchen. "Thanks for the advice the other night. It worked. She liked the scarf." He stroked the cat's back.

Duke squirmed, and Jake sat him on the floor. "How about shrimp for breakfast?"

The sleek gray feline licked his mouth as if in anticipation.

Jake opened the can, scooped it into a bowl, and set it on the mat. "Eat up."

He made it to the small house that served as an office for the private investigators in thirty-three minutes. Not bad, considering he spilled coffee on his shirt and had to change.

The smells of freshly baked blueberry muffins and coffee met him at the door—along with Sam.

"Have you heard from Mac?" His nose drew him toward the kitchen.

"I got a text this morning. She made it without a hitch, and they're having a good time." Sam yanked him off course into her office. "I've got the video ready for you to view—the tapes from the pipe factory?"

"Great. Where's Miss P? I could use one of those muffins and a mug of coffee."

"I'll get them for you. Miss P went to our post office box to get the mail."

Sam pushed Jake into a chair in front of her computer and pulled another alongside him. She pressed a few keys and the screen lit up.

"There's Eleanor arriving with the man Mac told you about." Sam pointed to the screen.

Jake nodded. The image yielded little information. He could guess at his height and possibly his weight, but that was about it. "Let's see the next one."

Sam loaded that one onto the computer.

"The man's not with her." Jake sipped his coffee and watched as Eleanor put her suitcases into her trunk.

"No—"

The front door opened.

"I'm back with the mail, Samantha. And a box for Mackenzie."

"What is it?" They abandoned the video and went into the conference area.

"I have no idea."

"Let's open it." Sam slit the box open with scissors and lifted a container of milk chocolates out. She looked at Jake. "Did you send her something?"

"Not me." A flash of jealousy overwhelmed his reason. Maybe she would have liked those better than a scarf.

"Don't go getting all macho. Let's see who did."

She'd read his mind again.

Sam extracted the card. "Thank you for all you've done. Connor Davis." She licked her lips. "Yummy. I'm going to text her and see if we can open it."

"Samantha." Miss Freebody straightened. "Connor Davis meant those for Miss Love."

"She won't mind. We're partners. We share." Sam's thumbs raced over the tiny keyboard. As she waited for a reply, she opened the box and selected one of the candies.

Her phone rang as she was lifting it to her mouth. "You didn't have to call. A simple yes or no would do, Mac."

"Don't eat those." The urgency in Mac's voice filled the room. "Connor would never send me milk chocolates. He knows I like dark chocolate."

Jake pulled a tissue out of a box nearby and snatched the candy from Sam's grasp. "Give me your phone and go wash your hand. Now." He stared at the box of candy. "Mac, he wouldn't send the wrong ones by mistake?"

"I guess he might, but let Ms. P analyze one before eating any."

"Will do." He pushed the box toward Miss Freebody, who placed it in a large baggie. "How are you?"

"Good. My sister, Kate, and I are going shopping and out for lunch today." She paused. "I'm glad you're there with Sam.

Let me know what Miss P finds out about the chocolates. See you soon."

"I HAVEN'T HEARD from Connor Davis since that day in the park." Mac strolled along next to Kate. She stopped to admire a sweater in a store window. "Do you think I'd look good in that color?"

"Yeah, but your budget would take a hit." Kate put her arm through Mac's and eased her away from the storefront. "Come on. There's a store down here that's got great clothes and is better on the pocketbook." The two women resumed walking. "So, you don't think Connor sent the chocolates?"

"No." Mac bit her lip. "Not just because he knows I like dark chocolate, but because I can't see him doing something like that."

"Then who did?"

"Got me." Mac stopped and looked at her sister. "But I came here to forget all that stuff, and today, we're shopping. So, let's shop."

"I'm with you. I love spending someone else's money." Kate rubbed her hands together.

"You're not going to buy anything?"

"Of course not. I'm just a poor lawyer's wife." Kate pulled Mac into a boutique. "Let's start here."

Several hours and packages later, Kate leaned against the outside of a building. "I'm done. How about lunch?"

"Sounds good. I only have one more thing. I want a T-shirt for Sam. I'll meet you at the restaurant." Mac dashed across the street to the shop where she'd spotted the shirt she wanted. Her phone rang.

"Hi, Sam. Do you know anything more about the

chocolates?" Mac grabbed the T-shirt she wanted and checked the size.

"Not yet, but Miss P and I had a breakthrough in the robbery case."

"Great. Hang on a minute." Mac handed the cashier some money and took her change. "Okay. What did you find?"

"All the burglaries happened in towns where the Missouri River Runner train stops."

Mac took the bag and pushed her way outside. "Say that again."

"He's doing the burglaries in cities with train stations."

"Eleanor must have found out." It was all clear to her now. "She knew who it was. That's why the thief killed her."

"What are you talking about?"

Kate waved to Mac from across the street. "I need to go. Talk later." No traffic. Mac stepped off the curb.

"Look out." A shout from behind and a shove. No time to tuck and roll. It was over in an instant. A black truck hurtled past within inches of where she lay face down. A man lay on top of her.

"Get off. I can't breathe." Sharp pain in her knees and elbows.

He shifted and rolled off. Hands helped her and the man to the curb. Her packages lay crushed on the pavement where they had broken her fall and kept her face from hitting the asphalt.

Thank You, Jesus.

"Thank God this gentleman pushed you out of the way." Kate knelt beside her,

Mac took a deep breath to calm her nerves and turned to the man sitting next to her.

"Dr. Ulrich?"

He tilted his head at her. "Miss Love."

Kate looked at Dr. Ulrich. "I can't thank you enough." She put an arm around Mackenzie.

"I'm only glad your sister wasn't hit." He eyed Mac. "May I take a look at your knees?"

Mac pulled her pant up above her knees.

"Concrete scrapes like we got when we were kids." He gently examined her elbows. "The same here. They'll sting but aren't serious." He smiled at her.

"How about you?" Mac said. "Are you okay?"

"Yes. One knee is all." He raised his pants leg. "I'd say we were both very fortunate. Do you feel able to stand?"

Ulrich and Kate helped Mac to her feet. He gave her arm a quick squeeze before releasing it.

"We were going for lunch. Would you care to join us?" Mac said.

"Thank you." He brushed off his clothes. "I'd like that."

Mac waited until they were seated and had drinks before answering the question in Kate's eyes. "Dr. Ulrich was with Connor Davis the day someone killed Connor's wife. He was—is—his alibi, and that's how we met."

"Please call me David." He smiled, his handsome tan face crinkling in all the right places. "When Connor was first arrested, I was away on a mission trip and out of pocket. I had no idea he'd been accused of Eleanor's death." He took a drink of his lemonade. "I was sent back when I contracted a fever and lapsed into a coma for several weeks."

"I tracked him down at a hospital in D.C., but they wouldn't let me speak to him." Mac smiled at him. "But he recovered—"

"And saved my friend just in the nick of time." He gave a slight bow.

"Like you saved me just now. Did either of you get a look at the driver or notice anything about the truck?"

"I was too busy being your knight in shining armor."

"My eyes were on you, sis." Kate laid a trembling hand on Mac's. "But the truck came out of nowhere. Do you think—"

"No." Mac squeezed Kate's hand. "Just a man in a hurry." Or was he? Best keep her doubts to herself.

"Connor told me you've been looking into Eleanor's murder." David leaned toward Mac. "Have you made any progress?"

Something was off. She held her tongue.

"No." She took a drink of iced tea. "We're thinking of dropping the case." What made her say that?

The doctor relaxed into his chair. "If it's not going anywhere, maybe it would be wise." He checked his watch and pulled some bills from his wallet. "I need to go, but let me pay for your lunch."

"No, no," the women said in unison.

"I insist." He held up a hand. "Here's my business card, Mackenzie. Next time you're in town, I'll take you to dinner."

"That would be nice, but I should be the one taking you to dinner." She studied the man before her. An idea flitted around the edge of her mind, but this wasn't the day to catch it.

After he'd left, Kate raised an eyebrow at her sister. "He's nice. Is he married?"

"I don't know."

"You should find out."

"I will." But why she felt the need to know was a mystery to her. Just like why she was sure she would have dinner with him soon.

CHAPTER 10

Her time with Kate had passed so fast, and once more, Mac sat on the train. Only this time, she had two pieces of luggage—the one she came with and the one borrowed from her sister to hold all her purchases. She couldn't help thinking of Eleanor. What did she do when she went shopping in Kansas City? Bring an empty bag with her? Probably. Mac should have thought of that.

The morning sun reflected off the metal and glass high-rise buildings as the train left the big city. About nine-thirty, the train pulled into Warrensburg, the second station after leaving Kansas City. Mac leaned her head against the window and watched as a man and woman boarded.

All her senses snapped to attention. When the man reached for the bar to pull himself up, he used his left hand— half his pinky finger was missing. The rest of him didn't seem to fit the description given by Leonard Reese, their initial witness. Could there be two men with the same deformity?

She stared at the door into her passenger car, but they

didn't appear. What should she do? She got up and snatched a newspaper lying on a seat nearby.

The next car was a café car, and the couple was sitting at a table on the left. Mac made her way to the counter and ordered a coffee. She took a seat close to them and opened the newspaper. From snatches of their conversation and their body language, she guessed they were acquaintances and not romantically involved.

His height and weight could fit with the man Leonard told them about, but this man was much younger, with no beard and wispy blond hair on his head. Of course, he could have used a disguise when he was with Eleanor.

The woman rose when the loudspeaker announced the train was approaching Jefferson City. Mac panicked. If the man got off, she'd lose him. Her luggage was in the other car. She returned to her seat and watched for him to depart from there.

The woman left the train at Jeff City, but there was no sign of the man. Should she see if he was still in the café car or stay put? Her mama would tell her to trust God and pray. So that's what she did.

Five minutes passed. The door to Mac's carriage opened with a whoosh, and there he was. He took the seat across the aisle from her. *Dear Jesus.* Her heart pounded in her ears. This might be her only chance to talk to him, but how to start? *Hi. Did you kill Eleanor Davis?* She suppressed a nervous giggle.

"You look so familiar to me." The man smiled at her. "Do you live in Kansas City?"

"Pardon me?" She swallowed the quiver in her voice.

"I asked if you live in Kansas City. You seem familiar."

"No. I'm from Washington." With a start, Mac realized they had run into each other—literally. "I may look familiar to you because I mowed you down in the Kansas City Station three nights ago when I turned unexpectedly."

"You're the one." He laughed. "I wondered who to send my doctor's bill to."

"Oh, no. Were you hurt?"

"No. Just kidding." He placed his right hand on his chest. "I'm Gary Wallace."

"Pleased to meet you." Mac stuck out her left hand to shake. "Mackenzie Love." Would he show her his finger?

"Forgive me if I don't shake. I injured my left hand the other day, and it still hurts."

"Oh, dear. How did you do that?" Mac worked to put honest concern into her tone and face.

"I repair large machinery, and I got careless." He shrugged.

"Farm machinery?"

"No, for factories. Presses and die cutters. Things like that."

"You must be very smart." She gave him her best smile. Playing to a man's ego was not her style, but if it meant finding Eleanor's killer ... "Do you have to travel a lot?"

He nodded. "My territory runs from St. Louis to Kansas City."

"The same as the Missouri River Runner. How fun. You can ride the train to work."

"Yes. It's the perfect job. My next assignment is at the brewery in St. Louis."

"How long will that one take?" She widened her eyes at him.

"Shouldn't be more than a few days. Then I'll head for home."

She gazed out her window. How could she ask him about Eleanor without spooking him?

"What do you do?" he said.

Should she tell the truth? "I have a small business in Washington. Nothing as exciting as your job."

"A boutique?"

"Yes." She crossed her fingers mentally. "In fact, one of my ladies was a regular on the train. She loved shopping in Kansas City. Maybe you ran into her? Eleanor Davis?"

Fear flickered across his face so fast that if she hadn't been watching, she would have missed it. But it was there. He knew Eleanor. Now he wore a look of concentration.

"The name rings a bell, but I don't think I know her." He snapped his fingers. "Hang on. Was she the poor woman who was murdered a few months ago?"

"Yes. It devastated everyone who knew Eleanor. I was hoping you may have talked to her on the train. Maybe you saw her with someone or saw something that could help us figure out who killed her." Mac wiped a nonexistent tear from her eye. "Her husband has been cleared, so her killer is still out there somewhere."

"I'm sorry. I wish I could help."

"Thank you." She reached across the aisle and touched his arm. "You've been so kind to listen to me. This is my stop." Mac pulled her bags from the overhead rack.

After the train stopped at the Washington station, she stepped into the aisle and looked at Gary. "Safe travels and God bless."

"Thank you." He flashed her a crooked smile.

WHERE WAS SAM? Mac paced in front of the station. They needed to act on her information as soon as possible. She spied Jake's police-issued sedan making its way toward her. He pulled to the curb and came around to stow her luggage in the trunk.

"I saw pinky finger man on the train." She couldn't wait

any longer. "His name is Gary Wallace, and he lives in Kansas City."

Jake paused as he reached for the door handle. "You talked to him?"

Mac nodded.

"I can't believe you did that." He glared at her.

She slid into the rear seat, and he slammed the door. Why was he acting so ugly?

"What happened?" Sam turned to peer at her.

"I talked to—"

"No." Jake peeled away from the curb. "We'll discuss this at the office."

Sam raised her eyebrows at Mac and faced front.

Mac stared out the window, her body stiff except for her chin, which trembled uncontrollably. Why was Jake so angry? All she'd done was talk to the man. At least she'd discovered more information about him. That should count for something.

She should be the angry one, not Jake. She glared at the back of his head. This was her case, not his. Hers and Sam's. The only opinion that mattered was Sam's. Her chin stopped trembling.

Jake's car bumped over the curb into the office driveway.

She reached for the door handle before remembering police cars didn't have handles in the rear. "Can you let me out?"

He opened her door.

She strode to the rear of the car.

"Go inside. I'll get your luggage."

"I can do it." Mac stiffened.

"Not until I unlock the trunk. Go inside."

"Come on." Sam took her arm.

Mac stomped up the walk. "I love you, but I'm so mad at your brother I could eat a porcupine."

"I know." Sam linked her arm through her friend's and pulled her inside.

"Good to see you, Mackenzie." Miss Freebody peered at her over her glasses. "Is everything okay?"

"It's fine, Miss P." Mac tossed her purse on the sofa. "I talked to pinky finger man on the train." She sat at the table.

"You did what?" Sam plopped into a chair next to her.

"You heard her." Jake dropped her suitcases inside the door and stomped across to the women. "I still can't believe you did that."

Mac pushed away from the table and stood to face Jake. "And I still don't understand why you're so upset."

"One minute you're telling me he may be a killer, and the next you're talking to him, telling him who knows what." Jake took a step closer to her. "That's his M.O. He meets women on the train. But you're not just any woman. You're the woman investigating the murder of Eleanor Davis."

"He didn't know that." Mac planted her hands on her hips.

"Think back over the conversation." Jake's voice lost its angry tone, and his eyes held a look distinct but equally intense.

She dropped her arms to her sides. "He said I seemed familiar to him, and it turned out I'd bumped into him at the Kansas City Station when I arrived."

"Do you think he was following you?"

"No ... at least, I don't think so." Mac rubbed her forehead. "I didn't get that feeling at the time."

"Did you tell him your name, where you lived, what you do?"

"I lied about my work. I said I owned a boutique." Which would be easy to check. She'd been a fool. She collapsed into the chair. "I asked if he knew Eleanor Davis. When I did, there was an instant of fear in his eyes."

"So, he knows he's in the frame for her murder." Jake let out a sigh.

Mac placed her elbows on the table and hid her face in her hands. What had she done?

"My dear, I have no doubt you did what you thought best." Miss P laid a hand on her shoulders. "Let's concentrate on what knowledge you gained from your talk."

Mac grabbed a tissue and wiped her cheeks. "His name is Gary Wallace. He lives in Kansas City, works as a heavy machinery repairman, and his present job is in the brewery in St. Louis. He'll be there for a few days."

"That's quite a lot." Miss P finished writing on her notepad. "Did he get on the train in Kansas City?"

"No, he boarded in Warrensburg with a woman. She got off in Jeff City. That's when he came back into my car and ... well, you know the rest." Mac's gaze landed on a piece of paper in front of her. "What's this?"

"That's part of what I was telling you about on the phone the other day." Sam scooted closer to Mac. "We began charting patterns surrounding the burglaries." She pointed to a column. "Like the fact that they've all taken place in cities where the Missouri River Runner stops."

Mac's pulse quickened.

"Do you think there might be a connection?" Miss Freebody joined them.

"Yes." A surge of fresh energy ejected Mac out of her chair.

"Take it easy." Jake stepped in front of her. "What do you mean?"

"What if Gary Wallace is the burglar, and Eleanor figured it out?" Mac sidestepped around Jake. "That could be his motive for killing her."

"When was the burglary in Washington?" She hurried to the table.

"The owners didn't realize it until they got home on Friday —the day after Eleanor left for Kansas City." Sam's eyes widened. "Mac, do you think—"

"He did the job on Wednesday night, and Eleanor gave him a ride to the train on Thursday."

"But how did he know her?"

"He'd met her on the train before, and she gave him a ride to his hotel."

"How do you know that?"

"I don't, but I bet if we can get the train records, we'll find out that Eleanor came back from Kansas City on Tuesday or Wednesday and returned on Thursday." Mac snapped her fingers. "And I think I know why." She stepped close to Jake and tapped him on the chest. "The important thing now is, are you ready to help me catch a burglar?"

CHAPTER 11

"Depends." How was it this woman could make him so angry one minute and get his heart racing the next?

She moved away, and it was all Jake could do not to pull her back.

"If I'm right, there was a robbery in Warrensburg last night, and the woman I saw today gave the thief, Gary Wallace, a ride to the station to catch the train to St. Louis. Just like Eleanor did in April. Only then he was going to Kansas City."

"If that's true, I need to get in touch with the police in Warrensburg." Jake pulled his phone from his pocket. "They'll need to do some checking." He stepped into Sam's office and closed the door. "Chief, I've got a situation here."

"Not again, Sanders."

Jake related events to his boss.

"How sure are you about this?"

"I'm not sure about the murder." Jake combed his fingers through his hair. "But the idea of this Gary Wallace as the burglar makes

"I'm friends with the chief in Warrensburg. I'll tell him what we know and offer our help, but ..."

"Maybe Detective Young could do some digging into Wallace? Find out who he works for and his schedule for the last six months. If we could match the dates he was in the towns with the burglaries, that would go a long way."

"I'll get him on it right away."

"Thank you, sir." Jake punched End and rubbed the back of his neck. Now to face Mac. She waited for him right outside the door.

"What did they say?" Small lines edged her chestnut eyes.

"I spoke to the Chief. He'll speak to Warrensburg."

"But—"

"It's a different county. We can't go barging in, Mac."

She paced around the reception area. "I didn't think of that." She gnawed on a fingernail. "There must be something we can do."

"Detective Young will find out who Gary Wallace works for and match his schedule to the burglaries."

Miss Freebody sorted papers into stacks. "Is there any way to find out if this man has approached other women on the train?"

"How about flyers at the train stations?" Sam said.

"Good idea." Mac paced. "But I think that's got to wait until we catch him, or at least get him in for questioning."

"Let's look at the timing." Jake walked to the table. "What burglaries have occurred since Washington in April?"

"Here's the list."

"Nothing in May. In June, Sedalia, discovered on the second Saturday." Jake ran a finger down the paper. "Skipped July. Jefferson City was in August, discovered on the third Sunday."

Mac came next to him. "The days they were discovered

don't tell us much. He may have broken in and stolen the goods days before."

"That's true," Sam said. "How can we tell?"

"We can't. We need to catch him and bring him in." Mac's stomach growled. "Miss P, do we have anything to eat around here?"

"Excellent idea, Mackenzie." She headed for the kitchen. "Sam, I could use your help."

An awkward silence fell over the room. Mac moved to the window, taking her warmth with her. "I'm sorry I jumped on you like that."

"I was an idiot. I didn't think." Her shoulders slumped.

"No." He crossed to her. "You're one of the smartest people I know. But I'm concerned about your safety. I ... you're my friend." He yearned to pull her into his arms, but how would she react?

She gazed at him, a soft smile on her lips. "Your friend?"

His heart pounded in his chest.

"The food is here." His sister, Sam, appeared with a platter of sandwiches and almost tripped on the area rug.

The moment vanished. Jake hurried over to rescue the plate of food. He licked his lips. "What are the rest of you eating?"

"Put it down, bro." Sam chuckled.

Miss P distributed paper plates and napkins. A bowl of chips rounded out their simple meal. And the usual iced tea to drink. "It isn't much, but it should sustain you until later."

"You are a gem, Miss P." Sam bowed in her direction. "I'm going to do some web searching of my own." She carried a loaded plate and a glass of tea into her office.

From across the table, Mac took a bite. She stared in his direction, but it was clear she wasn't focused on him. She was so beautiful—inside and out. If Gary Wallace hurt her ... his hands curled into fists.

AFTER THEY CLEARED THE MEAL, Mac walked to the end of the conference table where Miss Freebody had stacked her folders. "Miss P, walk me through how you organized your papers."

"Here are the individual files on each burglary." The older woman placed a hand on a neat mound of manilla folders. "These—" She touched two smaller piles. "—contain data I gathered to determine any patterns, and my conclusions."

"Perfect. I want to read through everything you've been doing." Mac stacked the piles together and carried them toward her office.

"I'll go home to work in my lab." Miss P said.

Mac stopped. "With everything else, I forgot to ask if you'd had time to analyze the candy."

"Not yet. That is my first priority this afternoon." Miss P picked up her purse. "I'll see you in the morning."

"What are you going to do, bro?" Sam stepped out of her office.

"I want to check in at the station." He pulled on his ear. "The question is, can I trust you two to stay put for a while?"

"Go." Sam gave him a shove. "We'll be good."

"Maybe I should go with you." Mac shifted the load in her arms.

"No way, girlfriend." Sam put a hand on her elbow. "Get out of here, Jake, while I have a grip on her."

"Let us know if you find out anything," Mac called over her shoulder as the door closed.

After scowling at Sam, Mac dropped the files on her desk, settled into her chair, and opened the top folder.

If only she'd known earlier Jake was going to the police station, she'd have come up with a good reason she should ride along. She sighed and reached for the top file once more. All the items stolen weren't the costliest pieces in the homes, but they were easily transportable—small enough to fit into a briefcase. Another fact that supported Wallace being the thief and using the train for transportation.

She had to admire his nerve. He'd do the job one night and then wait to board the train until the next afternoon, or possibly even a day later. All the time, the stolen goods were sitting in his luggage. He could have had something tucked away in his briefcase from his job the night before in Warrensburg while she was talking to him. A cool set of nerves. Especially if he knew who she was.

And all the while, she thought she was conning him.

But did he have the nerve to commit cold-blooded murder?

Her cell phone sprang to life. It was Jake.

CHAPTER 12

"**D**o you have him?" Mac jumped up and ran into Sam's office, motioning to her phone.

"No." Jake's voice filled the room. "But we heard from the Warrensburg police. You were right. There was a burglary last night. The owners came home today, and they wouldn't have noticed it except the police contacted them."

"What did he steal?"

"A ring." The crinkle of paper came over the phone. "A sapphire with a circle of diamonds in a gold setting. We've been in touch with the St. Louis police, and they're checking with known fences and pawnshops."

"We're closing in on him." Mac grinned at Sam.

"Maybe. Detective Young can't find any records of a Gary Wallace that fit the description of the man you met on the train."

"What about train tickets?" A chill ran through her. "He must have bought a ticket."

"Not under that name."

"Isn't he at the brewery?" Her chest tightened. She knew what Jake was about to say.

"The brewery never called for anyone to come work on their machines."

"Have Detective Young get in touch with the top ten firms that service factories and ask if they have anyone with half his pinky finger missing on his left hand." She rubbed her neck. "Get them to send photos of any employees that match that description."

"I already thought of that. He's working on it."

"Good. Thanks."

"Anything else ... boss?"

Ouch. "Sorry. I didn't mean it the way it sounded."

"Too late." Jake chuckled. "It's okay. I get it. By the way, the video at the pipe factory doesn't help. The man wore a hoodie and didn't look up. Why don't you go on home? Things will seem better in the morning."

She pictured the stack of folders on her desk without enthusiasm. It'd been a long day. She could use the rest. "I think I will." She exchanged a look with her friend and partner. "What do you say? You ready to call it a day?"

"Sure." Sam closed her computer and pushed back from her desk. "Alan will be thrilled to see me home earlier than expected."

"You're blessed, Sam." Mac did the circuit, turning off lights and checking windows.

"I know it. You could be too if you'd try." Sam grabbed a broom and began sweeping.

"What does that mean?"

"I've seen the way my brother looks at you and you at him."

"I think you're imagining things. Today he told me I'm his friend." But there was something—a connection for just a moment. Mac smiled.

"What are you smiling at?"

"Nothing. I'm not sure it's such a good idea for your brother and me to get together. What if one of us didn't like the other? Then you're caught in the middle."

"All I care about is that you're both happy—whether together or with somebody else." Sam put the broom in the closet. "I'd only pout for a few months."

Mac laughed.

"By the way, our fridge and cupboard are nearly empty."

"I'll take the trash out, and tomorrow, we can both go to the store." Mac grinned at her. "How does that sound?"

"You know how I hate going to the grocery store."

"Nobody likes a whiner." Mac pulled a trash bag from a box in the kitchen and walked into her office. She returned and headed for the back door. "I'll be back."

The wind was picking up. Gray clouds moved on the horizon. Mac lifted the lid on the large plastic trashcan. She caught movement from behind at the last second. Pulling her arms tight to her sides, fists ready, she turned to face her attackers. Two men in black pants, shirts, and ski masks.

"Hey." Sam rushed out the door. One of the men hit her with a club and she fell.

Rage seared through Mac. Distracted by Sam's moans, she hesitated. The other man punched her in the stomach. She stepped away from him, gasping for breath. A swift side kick from her connected with a yelp from her attacker. She moved in, arm cocked to deliver a jab to his throat. But they outnumbered her.

Sam's attacker got her in a chokehold. He pushed her toward the building. Lifting her feet, she pressed against the side of the house and thrust them both backward onto the ground. They rolled down the yard and stopped with the man on top, pinning her with his weight.

"No more warnings," the man whispered in a hoarse voice. "Next time someone dies." He pressed harder. Her lungs screamed for air. "Got it?"

She nodded. Sharp pain. Darkness.

When she came to, the men were gone. Sam had crawled over to her.

"Are you okay?" She inched her body closer to Mac.

"Other than my head—" which threatened to explode "—I'll live. How about you?"

"Same. I called Jake."

Mac groaned. More questions by the police and more poking and prodding by the EMTs. At least they gave her something for headaches. She pushed to her knees and let her stomach settle down.

Or maybe she'd rest here until ...

"Let me help you up." Jake reached for her.

She gripped his arms. "They said no more warnings. Next time someone dies."

"Let's get you taken care of first. Time enough to talk after that." He put an arm around her waist and helped her around front, where an ambulance pulled in.

"Sam?"

"She's on her way to the hospital."

How had she missed all that?

"You were asleep."

She raised her fingers to her head and traced the outline of a large bump above her left ear. A little further forward and it would have been lights out. Jake helped her into the ambulance, and it took off.

JAKE CHEWED on two antacids as he drove to the hospital. As much as he loved his sister and her friend, they were giving him an ulcer. When he reached the parking lot, he dialed the Chief.

"What now?"

"Two men attacked Mac and Sam tonight as they were taking out the trash."

"Are they hurt?"

"Blows to the head. Another warning that ups the ante." Jake ran a hand through his hair. "Stop or someone dies."

"I told you I don't want another person killed in my town, Sanders," the Chief said.

"Especially one of those two ladies. Do you understand me?"

"Yes, sir." Jake laid his head back and closed his eyes. What about catching the killer?

After a moment, he steered the car closer to the emergency exit and got out. Inside, Sam and Mac sat with bandages on their heads. Alan hovered over Sam. His heart lurched in his chest. These were his family—the people he loved most in this world. *Lord, guide me and give me the wisdom I need to protect them.*

"Anyone need a ride?" he said.

"I'll take you up on that." Mac stood. "Alan offered, but Sam needs to get home as much as I do."

"Bye, guys. I'll talk to you tomorrow." Jake took Mac's arm.

She eased it from his grasp. "I'm okay."

He studied her pale face. On the outside, she seemed so strong and independent, but he suspected underneath, she was hurting. He ached to take her in his arms. Instead, he opened the door of his car for her.

At least she let him do that much.

CHAPTER 13

S unlight blazed in through the window and hit her in the eyes. She hadn't drawn the curtains last night. Judging by the rumpled clothes she still wore from yesterday, she hadn't done much of anything.

Mac ran her tongue over her teeth. Yuck. She had a lot of maintenance to do before showing up at the office.

Clean hair and fresh clothes later, she felt almost human again. As Mac finished brushing her teeth and walked across her bedroom, she paused. The armchair in the corner welcomed her as it did every morning. Lately, she'd ignored it, but today she went over and sat down.

Her meditation corner consisted of a comfy chair, a lamp, and a small bookcase to hold her Bible and devotional books. She used to spend fifteen to thirty minutes or longer there every morning, but as the years went by, she'd found excuses for ignoring its pull.

Sitting in the chair was like putting on a comfy pair of pants. Mac picked up her book of devotions. The message for that day was based on Psalms, chapter sixteen, verse eight.

"I know the Lord is always with me. I will not be shaken, for He is right beside me."

The rest of the short devotional spoke about the importance of staying in communication with Him—something she hadn't done lately. And about giving the things she struggled with to Him. Something else she'd failed to do. She marveled at how often the devotional for the day spoke directly to how she was feeling at the time.

For Mac, being a private investigator was her mission in life. That probably sounded weird to most. To her, it was a way she could help others. But had she taken on too much with this case? She scanned the words before her again.

Another verse caught her eye. This one from Philippians, chapter four, verse six.

"Don't worry about anything; instead, pray about everything. Tell God what you need, and thank Him for all He has done."

So that's what she did. Prayed. Took it to God. And thanked Him.

She was ready to face the day. Almost. Where had she put her sunglasses?

Mac took a longer route to work, one that passed by Main Park. The trees sported leaves of many colors with a dark green pine or two to add contrast. She rolled her windows down and drove at a leisurely pace. The cool breeze played with her hair and filled the car with the earthy smells of fallen leaves. A good time to be alive.

After a turn onto Second Street, her office came into view on the right. Miss P's sedan sat out front, as usual. Back to work.

"I heard you had another mishap last night." Miss P eyed her.

"Yes." Mac related what happened. "Please be careful, Miss P. So far, Sam and I have been the only ones hurt, but who knows what they'll do next."

"I am always careful, my dear. Is Samantha sufficiently recovered from last evening to come in today?"

"I'm expecting her any minute." Mac walked into her office. The stack of files stood on her desk where she'd left them. She carried them out to the conference table once more. Might as well read them out there, where everybody had access.

"Whew." Sam came through the front door. "It's getting chilly."

"It's good to see you, my dear. How are you feeling?"

"Other than a splitting headache, I'm fine. Thanks for asking. What are you guys doing?"

"I'm getting the reading done I didn't do last night." Mac indicated the pile of folders in front of her. She narrowed her eyes at her partner. "Why? What's going on in that mind of yours?"

"Alan discovered it." Sam dashed into her office and returned with her computer. "There are websites for train enthusiasts with cameras at certain stations across the nation. I'm going to see if any of those have cameras at stations along the Missouri River Runner route and get footage that shows our guy."

"Go Alan." Mac high-fived Sam and turned to do the same to Miss P, who raised an eyebrow at her.

"Samantha, I'm brewing you a cup of chamomile tea."

"I need a cup of coffee before I tackle these files." Mac walked into the kitchen, where a fresh pot stood ready. *Bless you, Miss P.* As she took her first sip, her phone vibrated in her pocket. "Jake?"

"You and Sam need to get down here. Now."

Mac's body tensed at the urgency in Jake's voice. "What's going on?" But he'd hung up. Mac rushed to her partner. "Jake wants us at the station as soon as possible."

"Why?" Sam looked up from the table.

"He didn't say." Mac grabbed her purse. "But he sounded serious. Since you're in back, we'll take your car." She glanced at Miss Freebody. "You, too, Miss P."

The gray-haired woman straightened. "I believe I'll stay here. If you need me, call." She held up a hand. "Before you go, here is the partial print from the second note. You might want to take this with you." She handed a card to Mackenzie. "And my analysis of the candy showed that each chocolate contained a small amount of arsenic. Not enough in each piece to kill anyone, but if one ate several, one would feel the effects."

Mac's stomach churned. Somebody really didn't want her on this case. She folded the results of the chocolate candy analysis and put them in her purse, along with the fingerprint card. "We'll call you."

At the front door, Mac turned. "Lock the door behind us, and don't let anyone in."

"I'm quite capable of taking care of myself, Mackenzie." The thin woman folded her hands in front of her and peered at Mac over her glasses.

"Yes, ma'am." But they were no longer dealing with the typical small-minded idiots that threw rocks through windows. Far from it. And Miss P was no longer in her fighting prime. Maybe Mac should insist she come along? She studied her resolute friend. "Lock the door. For me. Please."

"I will take all the necessary precautions. For your peace of mind."

"Thank you." Mac hurried to Sam's car. In less than ten minutes, she would know why Jake summoned them to the police station. It would be a long ten minutes.

"Do you think Gary Wallace has killed someone else?" Sam stopped to let a mother and baby stroller cross the street.

"I hadn't thought of that." Mac drummed the door handle impatiently. "I was hoping he hadn't filed some sort of complaint against me."

"What would he have to complain about?" Sam threw her a quick look. "You didn't rummage through his luggage when he went to the bathroom, did you?"

"No." She'd thought about it, but the opportunity never came up. That was one thing she could cross off her list of possible offenses.

At last, they pulled into the parking lot. Mac waited for Sam before starting for the building.

Sam stopped her at the glass doors. "I just want you to know whatever happens in there—we're a team. I've got your back."

"Thanks, partner." Mac's heart swelled with affection for her friend.

"Let's rock and roll, girlfriend." Sam pushed through the doors into the pentagonal lobby made of glass and brick.

They continued through another set of double doors and up the stairs.

The woman at the desk recognized Sam. "I'll get Detective Sanders."

A few minutes later, Jake herded them to his desk. "I shouldn't have brought you here, but you did all the work. You deserve to be in on this."

"In on what?" Mac said through gritted teeth. He could be so frustrating.

"Gary Wallace walked into the police station this morning. Says he has something for us about the Eleanor Davis case."

Mac dropped into the chair by Jake's desk. "You're kidding."

Jake shook his head. "The Detective Sergeant has him in Interview Room One right now."

"Can we listen in?"

"Can we watch?"

Jake held up his hands. "Yes, but you must be quiet. Got it?"

Sam nodded her head, and Mac ran a finger across her pursed lips.

"Silence your phones."

Mac opened her purse. The fingerprint card and the analysis sheet caught her eye. "Here. Miss P found arsenic in the chocolates and could lift a partial print from the second note."

"Arsenic?" Jake paled. "We'll have to get the rest of the candies from her for evidence."

"She stayed at the office. I'll call her."

"Wait until after the interview. I'll send a car to escort her home." Jake rose and motioned them over behind his desk. "You're going to watch on my monitor with these headphones."

Mac and Sam sat side-by-side in front of Jake's computer. A room appeared on the screen with two men in it. Overhead fluorescent lights reflected off cinderblock walls painted cream with navy sound-reduction panels attached. No windows added natural light. Three chairs and a desk were the only pieces of furniture.

Gary Wallace sat facing the camera, and Detective Sergeant Hoover sat at the desk with his back to the camera. Mac donned the headphones. The movement of chairs, an occasional cough, and the Detective Sergeant's fingers tapping on the desk next to him were the only sounds.

She studied the face of the man she'd met on the train. Why had he come here? Were his nerves so cool that he'd chance a visit to the police to find out how much they knew? She rubbed her arms. If so, he'd be tough to trip up.

The door to the interview room opened, and Jake walked in.

CHAPTER 14

J ake pulled the third chair out from the wall.

"This is Detective Jake Sanders. He'll be conducting this interview." Detective Sergeant Hoover's words echoed in the small room. "He's been working on the Eleanor Davis case and the robberies we've had in the area lately. Are you aware of those?"

"I've heard about them in the news." Gary Wallace nodded. "Do you have any leads?" One corner of his mouth twitched.

"We're closing in on him." Jake studied the man's face. No reaction. "I understand you have information about the Eleanor Davis case."

"Yes. I should have come forward sooner, but I didn't want to get involved." He brushed a piece of lint from his pants and looked at the police officers. "My conscience got the better of me and I decided to tell you what I know."

"Which is?" Jake crossed his legs.

"I met Mrs. Davis on the train. We talked several times."

"When was this?"

Gary Wallace gave a half shrug. "February, March, April."

"Were you close?"

"If you mean did we have an affair? No." Wallace glared at Jake. "We became friends. She gave me a ride to my hotel when I had business in Washington. That kind of thing."

Jake nodded. "What kind of business?"

"I repair heavy machinery."

"Who were your clients in Washington?"

"I've done some work for Fischer Industries." Wallace's leg began to bounce. "Look, what does all this have to do with Eleanor's murder? Can't I just tell you what I know and leave?"

The ghost of an idea occurred to Jake. Could it be that simple? "Do you know Peter Fischer personally?" Jake gave Wallace his friendliest smile.

"I've been to his house for dinner. He's a very nice man."

Wallace's condescending smile spurred Jake on. His mind raced as he fought to keep his hands from shaking. "Then you know somebody robbed Mr. Fischer's home in April." Jake skewered him with his eyes. "You were in Washington during that time."

"Wait a minute." Wallace jumped to his feet. "I came here in good faith to tell you what I know about Eleanor Davis. Not to be accused of burglary."

"Sit down, Mr. Wallace." Detective Sergeant Hoover shot Jake a frown. "Detective Sanders didn't mean to imply that. Did you?"

"No, sir. Sorry, Mr. Wallace."

"Now." Detective Sergeant Hoover motioned for Wallace to continue. "Please tell us what you know about Eleanor Davis."

"She was making frequent trips to Kansas City to meet with a divorce lawyer," Wallace said, his words clipped.

Detective Young's voice sounded in Jake's ear. "Sorry to interrupt, but I need to talk to Detective Sanders. It's urgent."

Jake glanced at the Detective Sergeant, who also heard the message.

"Go on." Hoover waved a hand. "Mr. Wallace, would you like a bottled water or a cup of coffee?"

Jake met Detective Young in the hall.

"The St. Louis Police discovered the ring with a fence who identified Wallace as the man who gave it to him." Young handed him some papers.

A grin split Jake's face. "Good work, Vic. Let's see what he has to say now." He put on his stony face and reentered the interview room.

"Mr. Wallace, do you recognize this?" Jake produced a photograph of the sapphire and diamond ring stolen from a house in Warrensburg.

Wallace took the photo, a frown of concentration creasing his brow. "It's beautiful, but I can't remember ever seeing it."

"It was stolen from a house in Warrensburg this past week. We have a witness who will swear you gave it to him to sell."

A flicker of fear. "He must be mistaken."

"I don't think so. You were also seen getting on the train in Warrensburg the day after the ring went missing—traveling to St. Louis, where you gave it to the fence to sell for you." Jake scooted closer. "What do you want to bet if I show your picture to the man who owns the ring, he'll tell me you did some work for him, and you were at his house for dinner once? Or maybe twice?"

"Go ahead." Wallace took a deep breath. "I'll admit it. I've been to almost all their homes. That doesn't prove I stole that ring."

Jake moved a little closer. "Eleanor Davis's maiden name was Fischer. She grew up in this town. We all want to find the man responsible for her murder." He stared at Wallace.

"No." The man raised a hand. "You may think I'm a thief, but I'm not a murderer."

"Prove it." Jake leaned toward the man.

"When do they think she was mur ... died?"

"Sometime between twelve forty-five and one fifteen that Saturday."

Wallace pulled out his phone. After several attempts, his shaking fingers found what he wanted. "I just started a job in Kansas City. It was major and took me a little over a month to complete."

His alibi matched the timeline for the thefts. There were none in May and early June when he would have been working the Kansas City job.

"Why can't we find any record of you working for any of the top ten companies offering heavy machinery repair?" Jake leaned back in his chair.

"My real name's Greg Williams." He reached inside his jacket. "Here's my card."

"Greg Williams? Why tell us Gary Wallace?"

A wry smile appeared on Greg Williams's face. "The only reason I came in was that I knew Miss Love would report meeting me on the train. I gave her a false name." He shrugged. "I suppose you could say Miss Love was my conscience."

Jake had been right. Gary Wallace, or Greg Williams, knew who she was the whole time.

"We're arresting you on suspicion of committing burglary. The officer will read you your rights."

Jake believed him about Eleanor's murder, but he felt certain he'd caught the thief. They'd solved one case, but the murder remained open. Which meant Mac was still in danger. He cast a glance at the camera in the corner of the room. She'd seen and heard everything. He needed to get to her. "Do you need me here?"

"Where are you going?" Detective Sergeant Hoover stood.

"Mackenzie and Samantha are in the waiting room. I need to let them know."

"I guess we have all we need." He motioned for the officer standing in the hall. "We'll take his formal statement and charge him with the burglaries."

"Detective, I saw nothing in the news about the man Eleanor was dating," Williams said. "Was he ever a suspect?"

Jake returned to the center of the room. "What man?"

"I thought you knew. She told me she was seeing someone. He was married but in the process of getting a divorce."

"Someone in Kansas City?"

"No." He smirked. "Here. In Washington."

CHAPTER 15

Mac removed the headphones and stared at the screen in front of her. Their case had morphed before her eyes. With the new information and a new suspect, her mind swelled as if it were about to explode. She looked at Sam.

"This changes everything." Sam pressed a hand to her chest.

Dramatic as ever. But this time, Mac knew exactly how she felt. First order of business, find Eleanor's lover. "Time to rock and roll, girlfriend."

"We should speak to Jake before we leave," Sam said.

"I'm here." He surveyed the hall before shutting the door.

"What's all the secrecy about?"

"I told the Chief you were in the waiting room." Jake slipped into his chair behind his desk. "We never heard about an affair. Do you two have any idea who Eleanor's lover could be?"

"I'm not really in on the local gossip track." Sam looked at Mac.

"I'm persona non grata lately." Mac held up a hand. "Nobody tells me anything."

"We're really interested in what was going on six months ago. Before she died."

"That's true. Let me think." Mac stared out the window. Hoping for what? The name to be written in the clouds? No such luck.

Was Eleanor's lover the reason she and Connor separated? Who would she be willing to end her marriage for?

"She started dating Connor as a junior in high school." Mac turned to Jake. "They were inseparable. But there was a boy before Connor." She rubbed her temple. "What was his name? They were pretty serious for a while."

"Would your friend Ivy know?" Sam said.

"Good idea. If anyone's heard any gossip in this town, it'll be Ivy."

"Why's that?" Jake said.

"She waitresses for Cowan's restaurant, and I think the whole town goes there to eat at one time or another." Mac laughed. "It's amazing how people pay so little attention to the wait staff. They hear all sorts of things. Ivy has become our secret informant."

"She knows where the skeletons are buried?" Jake dumped the headphones into his bottom drawer and slid it shut.

"Not many skeletons in Washington, Missouri." Mac gave them a brief smile. "You guys have lived here long enough to know it's a quiet place. Eleanor's murder is the first in how many years, Jake?"

"At least ten. And then we lose two women from here on the same day."

"Eleanor and Mary Elizabeth." Mac looked at Jake. "You remember her, don't you? She was about your age."

"She must have moved before we got here." Jake nodded toward Sam.

"Is this the Mary Elizabeth found dead of a heart attack on the train?" Sam said.

"Yes. The same day Eleanor was murdered. Mary Elizabeth grew up here. We called her M.E. While we were in high school, she had an affair with a teacher. She got pregnant, and they ended up moving to Kirkwood, a suburb of St. Louis."

"What happened to them?" Sam placed a hand on Mac's arm.

Her friend always hoped for a happy ending. That was one thing Mac loved about her. "They got married, and last I heard, had three children."

"But there must have been trouble in paradise because Mary Elizabeth's sister is raising a stink about her death." Jake retrieved a paper from his desk.

"Faye?"

Jake nodded. "She's sure Mary Elizabeth's husband killed her—even though he was on a school trip all weekend. She's calling for a second autopsy."

"Whoa. Can she do that?"

"As long as Mary Elizabeth's husband agrees, and Faye pays for it."

"I thought I heard Mary Elizabeth had heart trouble." Mac furrowed her brow. "What makes Faye suspect foul play?"

Jake gave them *The Look.* What was up with that?

"Mary Elizabeth is not our concern." Chief Baker stood in the doorway. "Ladies. If you're done with my detective, I need him." He stepped forward.

Mac and Sam jumped to their feet.

"Thanks for letting us ... I mean, keeping us informed." Mac threw him a quick smile as she eased into the hallway.

Detective Young hurried past her. "Sir. Shots fired at the corner of Johnson and Second."

"Our office." Mac ran toward the stairs with Sam by her side. *Lord, not Miss P. Please, not Miss P.*

Jake caught up to them. "With me. It's faster."

They piled into his unmarked sedan and tore out of the lot, lights and siren blaring.

Mac and Sam sat in the rear, hands and hearts locked in mutual support and friendship. She prayed that hiring Miss P hadn't gotten her injured, or worse. When they arrived, Jake screeched to a halt and yanked the back door open.

"There she is." Mac ran to the ambulance in the driveway. Her heart pounded in her chest. "Miss P." It came out as a whisper. She cleared her throat and tried again. "Miss P."

"I'm fine, ladies. These young people are merely doing their job."

"Thank God," Sam said. "We were so worried about you."

The EMTs helped the older woman out of the ambulance. "She's fine. Wish we could say the same for your house."

Mac and Sam turned. A hideous slash of splintered wood and broken glass sliced across the front of the quaint little house. Mac trembled with anger.

"Our beautiful little office." Tears poured down Sam's cheeks.

"I know." Jake put an arm around his sister. "We'll find who did this."

"The house can be repaired, but how do you fix people's attitudes?" Mac pressed a hand to the ache in her chest. Maybe it was time to stop.

"You must never give up working for truth, Mackenzie." Miss P laid a hand on her shoulder. "One thug doesn't speak for the whole town."

"I'm just thankful you're okay." Mac gathered Miss P in for

a hug. "If anything had happened to you, this town would see what real revenge looks like."

"You don't mean that, my dear." Miss P peered at her over her glasses.

"No, but sometimes I wish I could take justice into my own hands."

"Justice belongs to the Lord, and you know that."

"Yes, ma'am." Mac glanced at their house. "And clean-up is for the rest of us."

"I'll get Leonard over to help." Jake picked up a house number from the lawn and handed it to Mac. "You'll need another window."

"Thanks for pointing that out." Mac grimaced.

"GO INSIDE." Jake would feel much better with the women indoors. He scanned Second Street for any vehicles that seemed suspicious. "See what damage they did in there. I need to talk to my guys."

He motioned to a couple of officers. "Start a door-to-door. Also, I need one of you to collect any shell casings or bullets. See if you can find tire tracks, skid marks, that kind of thing. You know what to look for. I'll be inside."

The threats against Mackenzie continued to escalate. Why? Was this someone afraid she'd discover who killed Eleanor or somebody who wanted revenge because, in his mind, she helped Eleanor's murderer go free? Who did he know in town that was that twisted? Two names sprang to mind. He pressed a number on his phone. "Detective Young. I'm going to text you a couple of names. Check to see where they've been today. I need it done right away." He pressed End.

"What damage do you see?" Jake stepped into the house.

"It appears whoever it was aimed high. The bullets came in the front at an angle and most lodged high in the back wall." Mac pointed to the holes. "We're lucky they missed the water heater and the furnace."

Jake imagined the trajectories of the shots. "They weren't aiming to kill anyone, but they could have." A flash of anger surged through him. He needed to keep a cool head, but he found it harder and harder to do.

"They had to have seen my car and Miss P's too. They would have thought we were here and shot anyway."

A nod was all he could manage. After a moment, he bit back his anger. "Where was Miss P?"

"She was in the kitchen. Praise God." Mac walked into the room at the back, and her eyes glistened with unshed tears.

He joined her and raised a tentative hand to comfort her. She slid her arms around him and pushed her face into his chest. Her quiet sobs shook her body, and he wrapped her in his embrace as naturally as if he'd been doing it all his life. "It'll be all right," he whispered into her hair until she calmed.

She loosened her grip and stepped away. "Thank you." She pulled a couple of paper towels from the rack and dabbed at his chest. "I made a mess of your shirt."

"No problem. It'll wash." What he wanted to say was, "It's worth it to hold you in my arms." But as usual, this wasn't the right time.

"You're a good friend." She moved back another step and wiped her eyes and nose.

An officer called from the main room. "Detective Sanders? We found a witness."

CHAPTER 16

"I 'm going with you." Mac splashed some water on her face and dried it with a kitchen towel.

"This is police business." Jake finished wiping his polo shirt with a special towelette he kept handy for such occasions. "The Chief wouldn't like it."

"He doesn't have to know."

As he crossed to the front door, Jake waved Sam and Miss P to their seats. "No. It's bad enough I've got one of you tailing along."

Mac gave her friends a thumbs up and followed Jake next door. She'd seen her neighbor, but they'd never spoken. She slowed. Considering the Connor Davis thing, maybe it wasn't such a good idea for her to accompany Jake after all. But, as Mama used to say, "If you worry, you don't trust. If you trust, you don't worry."

"Mackenzie Love, I can't believe you've had your office next to me for two years and we've never chatted." The middle-aged woman came across her yard and grasped Mackenzie by the hand. "I want you to know I think it's terrible the way some folks in this town are treating you." She patted Mac's arm. "You probably don't recognize me. I work at the historical society on Fourth Street."

"Mrs. White, isn't it?" Mackenzie grinned at her. "You helped me with research for one of our first cases." The woman was like a bloodhound sniffing out information from every potential source.

"Yes. How did that turn out?" The woman's bright eyes sparkled up at her.

"We resolved it to the client's satisfaction, thanks to you."

"Ma'am, I understand you saw something today?" Jake said.

"Sorry, Detective." Mrs. White straightened and faced Jake. "I saw a black pickup speed by." She pointed in the direction the truck went. "A man shot out his window into Mackenzie's office."

A chill ran through Mac, and she hugged herself. A black truck. Again.

"Could you see the driver? Was there anyone with him?"

"The windows were too dark to get a good look at him, but I think he was alone because he was the one who did the shooting. If he'd had someone with him, wouldn't the other man have had the gun?"

"Most likely, but not always." Jake nodded. "When was this?"

"About one. I was in the yard working in my flower garden." Mrs. White waved a hand behind her.

"Did you get a license number?"

Mac held her breath.

"No, but I recognized the dealer symbol on the back." The woman beamed at Jake. "They bought the truck in Kansas City at the same place I got my car."

Could it be the same truck that tried to run her down?

"Excellent. Please give your statement to my officer." Jake inclined his head toward the police officer. "You've been a big help."

"I'm happy I could." She took Mackenzie's hand once more. "I'm so glad no one was hurt. If there's anything else I can do, please let me know."

"Yes, ma'am." Jake touched Mac's arm. "We need to get back."

"Thank you." Mac gave Mrs. White a big smile. "I guess that's twice you've helped me with a case now. I may have to put you on the payroll."

She and Jake turned to go. Mac dreaded having to see their office once more—the gash across its front like an open wound to her heart. She kept her gaze down as they made their way to the lawn.

What was that noise? She snuck a peek. A man raked wood and glass fragments together from the yard while another swept debris into a pile on the porch.

The man on the porch took off his glove and wiped his forehead. "We live behind you on Johnson Street. The officer said it was okay. We heard the shots and wanted to help."

"Thank you." Mac's chin began to tremble.

"It's a big help. Thanks, guys." Jake steered Mac inside.

The smell of baking cornbread wafted through the entire house, and Mac's stomach rumbled. "Miss P is in the kitchen again."

"She's making soup." Sam handed Mac a dust rag. "You can help me finish cleaning the furniture. Start with your office."

"My office?" Mac stood in the doorway to her office and groaned. The floor had been swept, but glass and wood chunks covered her desk and everything on it. "How long do I have until we eat?"

"Get started and I'll come help when I'm done here."

"Leonard Reese is here," Jake said. "He'll put plywood over the windows again and putty the holes for now."

Mac caught sight of the two men outside loading trash into cans to be hauled away. Her heart swelled with gratitude for all the people willing to help. She leaned out the window. "When you get done, why don't you join us for dinner?"

"Thanks. We will."

She tossed her rag on her desk and went to tell Miss P there'd be two more—make that three with Leonard—for dinner. Maybe Miss P was right. Maybe the whole town didn't hate her after all.

MAC IGNORED the holes in the back wall that still needed attention and concentrated on the table before her. Steam rose from bowls of creamy potato soup and oven-fresh cornbread. The clank of spoons and sounds of voices talking and laughing were like medicine for her soul.

She looked at Sam. Tears rimmed her partner's eyes. Soft-hearted Sam, what must this be like for her?

Mac leaned over and patted her friend's shoulder. "We'll fix it up good as new."

Sam gave her a shaky smile.

"I hear you two are looking into Eleanor Davis's murder," the man from the porch said.

"We are." Mac wiped her eyes and mouth with a napkin.

"I moved here in high school. We were in the same grade."

"So, you know Connor too."

"Sure, but when I met Eleanor, she was going with somebody else." He took a drink and burped. "Excuse me."

Mac glanced at Jake. "Really? Do you remember who?" She kept her tone casual.

"Let me think. It wasn't too long after that she hooked up with Connor." The man stared at the ceiling. "Seems like his name was Bob? Rob? Something like that."

Mac's throat tightened. Robert Jackson. Mary Elizabeth's brother-in-law.

CHAPTER 17

The last spoonful of soup and bite of bread was consumed, and as the guests rolled out the door, Mac eyed the conference table.

"We need to regroup." She gathered empty bowls and headed for the kitchen.

"I agree." Sam collected plates and napkins. "This case has turned on its head."

"I'll help Miss P do the dishes while you two make a list of priorities." Jake squeezed her shoulder as he passed.

Mac's stomach fluttered. "I'll get my computer."

But when she got to her office, she could no longer ignore what had happened, and her spirits plummeted. The mess still covered her desk. She picked up the dust cloth and began sweeping the debris into piles.

"What are you doing?" Sam stood in the doorway. "This can wait, Mac. I'll help you."

Mac looked into the steady blue eyes of her friend. "Thanks, partner."

"We've got more important work to do." Sam pulled her back to the table.

Mac pulled a clean pad of paper and a sharp pencil in front of her.

Sam squinted at a spreadsheet pulled up on her screen. "I guess we can forget searching for the hotel Eleanor stayed at in K.C."

"For now."

"What about train tickets?"

"Detective Young has been working on those." Jake stood in the doorway to the kitchen, drying a bowl. "But since the railroad is government subsidized, it's taking a while to get anything. Same with security footage from the train station."

"Those things will help with your burglary case, but I'm not sure how much help they'll be in our case." Sam scratched her nose.

Jake disappeared once more into the kitchen.

"Let's prioritize our actions going forward." Sam pulled up a clean spreadsheet.

"I think we talk to Ivy and see if I'm right about Robert Jackson being Eleanor's boyfriend before Connor. If so, then interviewing Rob should be high on our list." Mac wrote on her pad.

"Talk to Ivy." Sam typed in.

"And interview with Rob."

"Who exactly is Robert Jackson?" Jake slipped into a chair beside her.

"He's Faye's husband. You know, Faye, who's lobbying for a second autopsy on her sister."

"I keep forgetting what a small town this is."

"Before we do anything, I suggest we go back to the original file and read it again." Miss P sat in the chair Jake pulled out for her. "Thank you, Jake."

"Good idea, Miss P," Jake said. "Where is the file?"

Miss P selected a folder from the pile near her. "I've read it several times. Perhaps one of you might want to read through it again?"

Mac picked it up and a piece of paper fell out. It was a screenshot of the text message entered into evidence.

"Eleanor typed this the day of her death but didn't have time to enter who the message was for or send it. The prosecution used this against Connor," Mac said, "stating it meant that he saw his wife with another man."

saw dnme xoxo ?

"Can you make sense of that?" Sam said.

"Yes. It says, 'Saw d and me kissing and hugging.'" Mac bit her lip. "What I want to know is if she's been having an affair with Rob, who's D?"

"Maybe she cheated on Rob with D, and he killed her." Jake yawned.

"That makes my head hurt. Too many twists and turns." Sam reached for the file. "Let's see what else we can find in here."

Sam read a page and passed it to Mac, who did the same and passed it to Jake. When the folder was empty, Miss P gathered the papers and placed them in order.

"Any new ideas?" Mac said.

Sam shook her head.

"I got nothing." Jake swiped his fingers through his hair.

"I'll call Ivy in the morning and set up a meeting." Mac scribbled a note on her pad. "I guess that's it."

"Not quite." He held up a hand. "We haven't talked about where you two will work while they repair your office building, and there are still the threats to deal with."

Mac slumped in her chair.

"Since they have caught the thief, I am free to oversee the repairs to the building," Miss P said. "I suggest you move your offices to your home, Mackenzie, for the time being."

"I second that." Sam raised her hand and smiled at Mac.

"I'll arrange for a squad car to be outside your house twenty-four-seven and escort you wherever you go." Jake stood.

Mac stifled a scream. Her tormentor remained free while her life became restricted. Where was the justice in that? *Be kind.* She heard her mother's voice in her head, and she smiled her thanks at Jake.

JAKE FOLLOWED Mac home and waited outside for the patrol car to arrive. "Call me if anything looks suspicious or you see a black truck around."

"Will do."

Jake cruised down the street, his mind on the day's events. He never expected Eleanor Davis's murder to lead to the solution of a string of thefts. What a small world. Of course, it would have been even simpler if Williams had killed Eleanor Davis. Then both cases would be solved.

But at least Greg Williams, or Gary Wallace, or whoever he was, gave them a lead. Jake turned onto his sister's street. Her house sat about mid-block. He peered out his window and saw her car tucked next to Alan's in their carport. Good.

Jake felt a pinch of envy. As happy as he was for his sister and relieved that she had someone like Alan taking care of her, he yearned for a special someone in his life too. Mac's face swam before his eyes, and he slowed.

Maybe he should tell her how he felt? Only, he wasn't sure himself. Best let it alone for now. He steered his car for home and his cat.

CHAPTER 18

"M iss P?" Mac pressed her phone to her ear and placed a hand over her other ear. "I can hardly hear you." Sounds of hammering and sawing overpowered the older woman's words.

"Is this better?"

"Much. Boy, they started early."

"Yes. I arrived at seven, and they were sitting outside in their trucks when I got here."

"Great." Mac gave Sam a thumbs up. "Did you need us for something?"

"A young lady is here. She wants to speak to you. In person."

"Who is she?"

"Mrs. Faye Jackson." What could Faye Jackson possibly want with them?

Mac muted the phone and stared at Sam.

"What now?" Sam paled.

"Faye Jackson wants to see us. Do you think it has anything to do with Mary Elizabeth?"

"I bet it does." Sam's eyes sparked with interest.

"What do you think? Should we see her?"

"Why not?"

"Miss P, send her over." After she hung up, she turned to her partner. "Are we ready to handle two death investigations at the same time?"

"Let's see what she has to say. We can always say no."

"Right." Mac straightened the papers on her dining room table and ran a hand through her long hair.

Sam slipped her feet into her shoes and examined her teeth in the mirror. "Do I look okay?"

"You'll do." Mac shouldered her out of the way and brushed some gloss on her lips.

The bell rang. "I'll get it." Sam opened the door. "Welcome, Mrs.—oh, it's you."

"Thanks a lot," Jake said. "Just checking to make sure you're okay in here."

"We're fine." Sam pushed him out the door. "Go away, bro. We're expecting a visitor."

"Who?"

Sam sighed. "Faye Jackson."

"Please tell me you didn't call Mrs. Jackson and—" Jake growled.

"No. She called us." Sam gave him another push. "Go."

Mac stood at the window as Jake stomped over to his car. He got behind the wheel just as a sleek silver sedan pulled into the driveway. Mrs. Jackson had arrived.

"Please come in." Sam ushered the platinum-haired woman to a spot on the sofa.

"I hate to bother you at a time like this." Faye Jackson crossed her long legs and worried her bottom lip with her teeth. "I heard about your office, and when I saw the damage, I was shocked. Who would do such a thing?"

"It's not as bad as it looks." Mac smiled at her. "Would you like something to drink?"

"No, thank you."

"Well, then. Why don't you tell us why you're here?" Sam held a small notebook in her hand.

"I know you're investigating Eleanor's murder, but did you know my sister died the same day?"

"We're sorry for your loss, Mrs. Jackson," Sam said.

"Thank you." Faye offered a practiced smile.

"Mary Elizabeth. A heart attack, wasn't it?" Mac cut a look at her partner.

"That's what the incompetent medical examiner, or whatever he is, said." Faye spat the words out in disgust. "I know she was murdered." She leaned forward. "By her husband."

"Do you have any proof?"

"That's where you two come in. The police think I'm crazy. Or they're too lazy to do anything." Her eyes burned with conviction. "I know he did it. I need you to help me prove it."

Mac studied the woman across from her. What should they do? If Eleanor and Faye Jackson's husband, Robert, were having an affair, he became their primary suspect. How could they take this case without jeopardizing the other one?

"What you're asking will involve a lot of time and energy, Mrs. Jackson." Mac stood. "Will you give Mrs. Majors and me a day or two to consider whether we can accept your case?"

"I understand." Faye smoothed her pants leg with one elegant hand. "Please sit down, Miss Love." A sad smile tugged at the corners of her mouth. "I know about my husband's supposed affair with Eleanor Davis."

Mac fought to keep her composure. She prayed Sam did the same. "I see."

"Robert assures me Eleanor came to him as a friend seeking advice."

"But he didn't tell you?"

"Eleanor begged him to keep their meetings a secret, but after a while, he told her either she allowed him to share their relationship with me, or he would have to stop seeing her."

"What did she say?"

"She said no. It ended well before Eleanor was murdered. Robert had nothing to do with her death." She lowered her head. "Still, I see where that could be a problem for you. I've convinced him to speak candidly with you and your partner to clear away any obstacles his involvement might present."

"Excuse us a moment." Mac motioned for Sam to follow her into her bedroom. After she closed the door, she turned to face her partner.

"This is nuts." Sam wrung her hands. "We've never dealt with anything like this before."

"You were the one who said we should hear her out. Do you want to back out?"

"No. But I need a moment to absorb what just happened in there."

"Sam, look at me." Mac stared at her. "Breathe. In. Out. We got this."

Sam rolled her eyes."So now you're the one who wants to take the case."

"Yes. And no." Mac chewed on her lower lip. "But this way, we're assured of an interview with Robert Jackson. We can wait to accept the case until after the interview. How about that?"

Sam nodded.

Mac led Sam to the living room. "We can't promise anything until we speak with your husband. After that, we'll let you know."

Faye Jackson stood. "Agreed." She shook hands with Mac and Sam. "He'll be here this afternoon."

They stood side by side at the window until Faye Jackson's car disappeared down the street. Jake exited his vehicle and strode toward Mac's house.

"Here comes trouble," Mac said.

"It'll be all right." Sam opened the door. "Hi, bro."

"Are you two going to fill me in?" Jake said.

"Nothing to tell—yet." Mac faced him. "We haven't decided if we're going to take the case or not."

"Her brother's coming to talk with us this afternoon," Sam said.

Mac gave her the evil eye.

"I want to be here." Jake stared at Mac.

"It's a private meeting." Mac stared back.

"This man may be dangerous. It's my duty to protect you."

"We can take care of ourselves."

"After all the rules I've broken and risking my job so you could be a part of things, you're shutting me out." Jake crossed his arms over his chest.

She didn't like it, but he had a point. Mac paced. "I'm concerned he won't talk with you here."

"What if I put a microphone somewhere and listen in from the next room?"

"Jake, please." Mac furrowed her brow at him. "We'll pass on anything that has to do with Eleanor's case. Or Mary Elizabeth's."

He sighed. "I'll be outside. If you need me, come to the window and act like you're swatting a fly."

BY ONE-THIRTY, they'd finished preparing for the interview with Robert Jackson. Mac ran a brush through her hair and dabbed on more lip gloss. Samantha spritzed herself with her latest scent, the one Alan bought her for her birthday.

A steel-gray sports car pulled into the driveway.

"Whoa." Sam gravitated to the front window as if pulled by an invisible force. "What a car."

"I don't remember seeing it around, do you?"

"No."

The door opened, and a man unfolded himself from the front seat. He wore khakis and a tan leather jacket, with the hint of a green collared shirt underneath.

"What's your initial impression?" Mac said.

"I can see why Eleanor would be attracted to him. He's tall, handsome, and looks like a nice person."

"The same could be said of his wife."

"True."

"Do you think it was like Faye said—a friendship and not an affair?"

Sam sighed. "I don't know. He's awfully good-looking, and they were an item in high school."

"Affairs make me sad."

"Me too." Sam put an arm around her friend.

"I know we're all human and we all make mistakes, but this case is shaking my faith in marriage. Are there any good marriages out there today? Marriages where both people take their commitment to each other seriously?"

"Yes." Sam turned to face her friend. "Alan and I do. Your sisters and their husbands do."

"What makes the difference?" She knew she could be trusted, but what about the other person? How could she ever be sure?

"In ours, and in your sisters', you know what it is. It's that third cord in the rope. Faith," Sam said. "Mac, when we do something wrong, we have to pay for our mistakes. Our job as private investigators is not to judge, but to help make sure some people are held accountable for their mess-ups."

"No matter what went on between him and Eleanor, Robert Jackson could help us find Eleanor's killer and make him pay for his wrongdoing."

"That's the plan. If he's not the one who shot her himself." Sam walked to the door. "Hello, Mr. Jackson. Come in."

"Mrs. Majors, Miss Love."

"Why don't we sit over here?" Mac indicated the sofa and chairs.

"Could we get this over with as quickly as possible?" He perched on the edge of the sofa. "I hated keeping my relationship with Eleanor from my wife. I'm trying to put it behind me and get on with my life."

Poor Eleanor. Mac studied the man in front of her. It seemed everyone wanted to put her behind them and get on with their lives. First her husband, and now her ex-boyfriend turned friend?

"We understand, Mr. Jackson." Sam sat back in an armchair and crossed her legs. "Would you begin by telling us about you and Eleanor in high school?"

He scooted back on the couch and folded his hands in his lap. "Not much to tell. We dated for a couple of years until she met Connor. Then that was that."

"She ended it." A statement, not a question. Mac gave him a tight smile.

He nodded. "I started dating Faye, and after college, we married."

"How long have you been married?"

"It will be eight years next January." A smile tugged at his lips.

"A long time," Mac said. "And yet, when Eleanor came back around, you chanced everything to meet with her and kept your friendship a secret. Or was it really an affair?"

He stilled. "Eleanor was a beautiful woman, but I love my wife. I could never—would never—do anything to hurt our marriage." He stared at the corner of the room. "Eleanor could be very persuasive, and I guess I felt sorry for her." He shifted his gaze to Mac. "But after a couple of months, I came to my senses. I told her I wouldn't keep our friendship from my wife."

"What did she do?"

"She cried and made me promise not to tell her anything we'd discussed. But I had to tell Faye some of it."

"When did you tell your wife about the relationship?"

"Immediately after it ended, and, thankfully, she forgave me. But when Eleanor was shot, I knew the police might eventually come around to me—that I could be a suspect." He scooted to the edge of the cushion again. "I did not kill Eleanor. I swear it. There was no reason for me to do that."

"We have information that she was traveling to Kansas City to consult a lawyer about a divorce and that there was another man in the picture. Do you know anything about that?"

"One reason she sought me out was advice about getting a divorce. She didn't trust any of the lawyers here."

"Why?"

"She didn't want Connor to know she was in the process until it was done. Because of their prenups."

CHAPTER 19

Mac and Sam exchanged a look.

"What about her prenups?" Mac eyed the man in front of her.

"I can't remember." Robert furrowed his brow. "She told me, but I wasn't paying much attention. By then, I knew I needed to put an end to our meetings."

"Do you know who she was consulting in Kansas City?"

"I gave her a list of five divorce lawyers, but I'm not sure if she contacted one of them or not."

"Text me the list, please." Sam gave him her phone number.

"On another subject, your wife believes her sister has been murdered by her husband." Mac looked up from her notes. "Do you agree with her?"

"I don't know." He scrubbed a hand down his face. "I'm pretty sure Mary Elizabeth was seeing someone behind his back, but I don't know if her husband knew."

"What makes you think she was fooling around on him?"

"Unexplained trips, calls she'd take in another room, that sort of thing."

"Would you say he's a violent man?" Sam said. "Had he ever hurt your sister-in-law?"

"My wife would know more about that, but I don't remember any problems."

Mac stood. "Thank you, Mr. Jackson. We appreciate you coming and speaking with us."

Sam got up and extended her hand. "Yes, thank you."

"Mr. Jackson, I think you should know we've been working with the police on both Eleanor's case and your sister-in-law's."

His lean face turned ashen. "I see." He squared his shoulders. "Miss Love, do whatever is necessary to clear my name and help you catch whoever committed these murders. I'm just thankful my wife trusts me."

"Please tell her we'll be in touch about her case."

Sam leaned against the door after Robert Jackson had gone. "Aren't prenups a matter of public record?"

"I'm not sure. We'll ask Jake."

They watched as Jackson sped away in his low-slung sports car. Jake crossed the lawn and entered the living room.

"How'd it go?"

"He only threatened us once, but it was with a knife. So we just pulled our guns and he backed off." Mac walked into the kitchen.

Sam giggled and closed her notebook.

"Very funny." Jake plopped on the couch.

"Would you like a lemonade or iced tea?"

"No, thanks."

"I'll take a water," Sam said.

Mac returned with a water bottle and a glass of iced tea. "Most of what he said wasn't much, but he did mention a prenuptial agreement between Eleanor and Connor. Are those public record?"

"Not always. I'll add that to the list for Detective Young."

"So far, you've given him lots of assignments without us hearing any results. Are you keeping them to yourself?" Mac took a sip.

"No." Jake raised a hand. "I promise. When I know, you'll know. The wheels of justice grind—"

"Exceeding slow, I know." Mac rolled her eyes at him.

Jake's phone rang. "Here he is right now. Any news?" Jake listened for a moment. "Okay. I got another thing for you to do. I'll text it to you." Jake smiled. "Same here."

His phone rang again.

"You're popular all of a sudden."

"Yes, sir." Jake glanced at Mac and Sam. "Yes, sir." He pressed End. "I need to leave. The Chief wants to meet. I'll get someone outside."

"Is everything okay, bro?"

"Sure." Jake hugged Sam and tipped his head at Mac. "Talk later."

A shiver went down Mac's spine. She had a bad feeling about this.

"I don't want to wait for Detective Young." Sam pulled out a chair in front of her computer. "If Eleanor and Connor Davis had a prenuptial agreement that's public record, I should be able to find it."

"Fingers crossed." Mac went to refill her iced tea.

Mac sipped her drink and thumbed through her notes. "If her husband didn't kill her, and Greg Williams, the thief, didn't kill her, and Robert, her friend, didn't kill her, who did?"

"We know the most common motives for murder are lust, love, loathing, and loot." Sam stopped scrolling. "Although I've also read that robbery, jealousy, and vengeance are the most common reasons one person kills another."

"Robbery fits with loot, jealousy with lust and love, and vengeance with loathing." Mac shrugged. "I'd say they're both right. The question is, what's the motive for Eleanor's murder?"

"If we consider vengeance or hatred as a motive, I suppose we should include Faye Jackson on our list of suspects. She could have been jealous of Eleanor's friendship with her husband."

"Wouldn't that be something?" Mac raised her eyebrows at Sam. "We help one murderer find another murderer. Maybe taking Faye's case wasn't such a good idea after all. Do you think she's hiding something under that calm exterior?"

"She's passionate and driven enough to force a second autopsy for her sister." Sam tapped a fingernail on her keyboard. "I'd say that makes her a force to be reckoned with, wouldn't you?"

"And asking us to help puts her in a position to learn what's happening with Eleanor's case too." Mac worried her bottom lip. Were they letting a fox into the henhouse?

"It's not here." Sam closed her computer. "Their prenups must not be public."

"Of course not. That would be too simple." Mac propped her head on her hands.

"I guess we could ask Eleanor's father. He probably knows."

"Do you think Jake would go with us? Maybe Mr. Fischer would feel better about talking to us with him along."

"I'll call him and see." Sam hit a number on her phone. After a moment, she looked at the screen. "He texted me. He's still in a meeting with the Chief and can't talk right now."

"In the meantime, let's get something to eat. I'm starving."

"You're always hungry." Sam laughed. "I don't know how you stay so slim."

"Do you think we should take the case with Faye or not?" Mac placed a slice of ham on bread.

"I'm not sure." Sam handed her the mayonnaise. "Why don't we sleep on it and see how we feel in the morning?"

"I agree. In fact, I'm not sure about Rob either."

"You think he lied to us?" Sam carried her plate to the table.

Mac followed. "Right now, I don't think we can rule out anybody but Connor and Greg Williams." She pulled her notes next to her. "We've got a list of motives. Let's put suspects with motives."

"Okay." Sam took a drink. "Lust/love. I guess Rob, if they were having an affair and Eleanor broke up with him instead of the other way around."

"Connor would be perfect, but he's cleared."

"We already paired Faye with loathing. Can you think of anyone else?"

Mac shook her head. "Loot. Again Connor, and again, not him for the same reason."

"I guess her brothers might kill her for loot. Her death increases each of their shares."

"True, but I know them. They've always been a close family, especially after their mother died." Mac studied her list. A weight settled in her stomach. "We may not solve this one, partner."

"Stop." Sam rose. "We're certified private investigators, and I have the paper to prove it. So, let's investigate."

"How about a nap first?"

"You nap, I'll clean up."

MAC STRETCHED, and her neck cracked. The couch wasn't the ideal place for a nap. "What's up?"

"I don't know." Sam stood by the front window. "The officer across the street left in a hurry. I tried calling Jake, but he texted he can't talk."

"Something big must be happening." Mac levered herself off the sofa and crossed the living room. "We'll find out soon enough. What time is it?"

Sam glanced at her phone. "Ouch. I need to get home. Alan and I have a date tonight." Concern clouded her face. "Will you be okay by yourself?"

"I'm meeting Ivy at Cowans for dinner. I'll let Jake know where I'll be."

"Tell Ivy hello for me." Sam's face cleared. "See you tomorrow."

Mac wasn't exactly truthful, but she didn't want Sam to cancel her date with her husband. Besides, she'd be fine. She pulled her phone from her purse. "Ivy? Are you free for dinner tonight?"

CHAPTER 20

"It's been a long time since we had a girl's night together." Mac raised her glass of iced tea to toast.

"Too long." Ivy clinked hers against Mac's. "I heard about your office building. That was horrible."

Mac scanned the restaurant. Things had changed a little. While there were still some glares, a few people greeted her and expressed sympathy for what happened. She gave Ivy a half-smile. "It'll get fixed. Thank God no one was hurt."

"Do the police know who did it?"

"Not yet. Do you know anyone with a black pickup?"

"Was that the car?" Ivy leaned across the table.

"It's possible, but keep this between you and me. Okay?"

"Sure." Ivy narrowed her eyes. "I can't think of one, but I'll keep a lookout."

"There's something else I wondered if you remembered."

The server brought their food, and Ivy bantered with her for a moment and smiled as she left. "She's a sweetheart. I'm so glad they hired her. Now I can get some time off."

"You deserve it." Mac took a bite of her burger.

"What were you asking me about?"

Mac swallowed and wiped her mouth. "Do you remember who Eleanor Davis dated in high school before Connor?"

"Rob Jackson. In fact, they were sort of engaged."

"Have you heard anything about them having an affair since she and Connor got separated?"

"Oh, yeah." Ivy grinned. "It fueled the gossip mill for quite a while."

"Why didn't I catch wind of it?"

"You're a P.I. now, honey. Face it. You're not one of the regular girls anymore." Ivy tapped Mac's hand with her finger. "But I'll always have your back, girlfriend. Anything you need to know, just come to me."

Mac barked a laugh. "I told somebody you were my secret informant."

"Oooh. I like that." Ivy wiggled her shoulders. "Makes me feel important."

"So, informant, who do your sources say ended the affair?"

"It didn't. As far as I know, it was moving and grooving right up until she died."

Mac leaned back in the booth. Had Robert lied to them and his wife? Or had the gossip mill got it wrong?

"But he would have ended it soon. He would never have left Faye." Ivy scrunched her brow.

"Because of her money?"

"No. Because she's pregnant—at least she was at the time." Ivy took a drink.

Mac stopped chewing. Another reason for Faye to want Eleanor out of the picture. "But she's so thin. What happened?"

"She lost the baby at two months. Rumor is she blames the stress of the affair."

"That's terrible." Mac spread the fingers of her hand over her abdomen.

"Speaking of pregnant and Faye, wasn't that awful about her sister, Mary Elizabeth?"

Mac nodded, not sure how Ivy made the connection.

"I heard Faye thinks that was murder too and is pushing for a second autopsy." Ivy gave Mac an expectant look.

"She does, and she is." That much was public knowledge, but Mac's obligation to a client kept her from saying anything more, and all this talk of affairs and miscarriages hurt her heart. Time to change the subject.

"Do you remember the trouble you used to get us into in high school?" Mac narrowed her eyes at her friend.

"Me?" Ivy protested. "I recall it was you who got us into trouble."

"I'm going to need some of Cowan's famous mile-high pie if I'm going to defend myself."

MAC HADN'T INTENDED to stay so long at dinner, but once she and Ivy began exchanging stories, the time flew by. And she'd forgotten to text Jake where she was.

The night smelled like autumn. Clouds covered the moon and stars, and even though it was early October, it felt like Halloween. Mac hurried up the sidewalk to her car, got in, and locked the doors. A text came through from Jake. He'd meet her at her house.

She pulled away from the curb and headed up Elm St. At Fifth Street, she glanced left. No cars in sight. But when she turned right, the black grill of a big truck filled her rearview mirror. She gripped the steering wheel and pressed the accelerator to the floor.

No use. The black in her mirror remained—the vehicle behind her matching her speed. She passed the turn to her house. The sign for Moe's Pizza flashed by in the darkness. A lonely stretch of fields separated the restaurant from a cluster of homes. Her heart leaped into her throat.

The terrifying sound of metal-on-metal and her car sprang forward, hurling her backward against the seat. She lost her grip on the wheel. As her body whipped forward, the airbag explosion caught her in the chest. The car spun out of control, flinging her sideways to the limit of the seatbelt. Trees and fields whirled past her at a sickening speed. She closed her eyes to control the nausea.

Finally, after what seemed like hours, the car stopped its mad dance. She lifted her head and peered out her side window.

The glare of headlights sped straight toward her. Mac stabbed the release button on her seatbelt. "Dear Jesus, help me." The belt sprang free. She clawed her way across the console. Her fingers grasped the door handle, and she threw herself against the passenger door.

It didn't budge. A primitive cry escaped Mac's mouth. "Abba." She curled into a ball and braced for impact.

"Mackenzie, are you all right?"

She opened one eye. The shadow of a figure outlined against bright light. Was this heaven? But she was still in her car. And in pain. She unfolded her body and began to shake.

"I can't get the door open," she said through chattering teeth.

JAKE SWEPT the beam of his flashlight over her shivering form. She was going into shock. He had to get to her.

"I've called an ambulance. Stay put until they get here." His heart pounded in his chest. "I waited outside your home. A 911 call came in about an accident on 5th Street, and something told me to respond. When I did—your car—crashed."

Two patrol cars and a fire engine arrived, sirens and lights ripping through the October night.

"Help me get the driver's door open." Jake motioned to one of the officers.

He should preserve evidence, but the urge to be near Mac overwhelmed him. With a screech of metal, the door gave, and Jake squeezed into the driver's seat next to her.

"I ..." Jake touched her hand with his finger. "Are you hurt?"

"Bruised where I scrambled over the console and," she raised a trembling hand to her chest. "Where the airbag hit me. How did you find me again?"

"Somebody called in an accident. I heard about it on my radio."

"Did they catch the jerk?"

"No." The corners of his mouth lifted in a brief smile, her anger a positive sign. She would be okay. "Did you see anything?"

"Just a dark grill. No headlights." She closed her eyes. "I'm tired."

"Mac, don't go to sleep." Where was that ambulance? Sirens sounded close by.

Jake brushed the hair from her face. A knot the size of a golf ball protruded from her forehead. He climbed out of the wreck and ran over to the ambulance.

"Get over there now. The driver's in trouble." Jake jogged after the EMTs, his stomach churning.

After several minutes, the firefighters forced the passenger side door open, and Mac was lifted onto a gurney, ready to be taken to the hospital.

"Are you coming, Detective?"

"I'll follow in my car."

He called Samantha on his way. "Get in touch with Mac's sisters and let them know." Worry settled like a weight on his chest.

"We'll meet you at the hospital," Sam said.

Jake raced across town, praying for Mac and for a clear path as he ran through stop signs and lights until he reached the hospital parking lot. There, he swung into a spot and sprinted for the ominous red sign glaring in the night. Sam and Alan stood outside the emergency room. A man in a police uniform, hat in hand, rose to his feet behind them.

Jake gritted his teeth. If he didn't need his job, he'd never speak to Chief Baker again. After all, it was his boss's fault Mac was in the hospital. If the chief had done his job in the first place, none of this would have happened.

"Steady, bro." Sam placed a hand on his arm.

She'd read his mind again. What would he do without her?

"Did you talk to her sisters?"

"Yes. They said to keep them posted. If we think Mac needs them, they'll be here." Sam glanced at Alan. "We thought it best to see what the doctor thinks first."

Jake nodded. Time to face the boss. The distance across the floor to his chief seemed like a mile instead of a few feet. "Sir."

"Detective." The balding man raised bloodshot eyes to meet Jake's glare. "I understand this was no accident. That Miss Love was the victim of a hit-and-run."

"Yes, sir." Was he being demoted?

Chief Baker shifted his stance and grimaced. "Can we sit?"

Jake pulled a chair over and sat. "Chief, before you say anything—"

"Be quiet, Sanders." The Chief raised a hand. He settled

into a chair and hung his hat on his knee. "I'm not happy about what I have to do."

Jake's heart sank. He'd worked so hard to get to detective. Maybe it was time to move. Start over in another department.

"I can see I made an error in judgment." The Chief ran a hand over his hat. "It's too late to stop Miss Love and your sister from investigating the Eleanor Davis case. The only thing left to do is join them." Chief Baker rose. "I'll give you what we have on the case. Find out who killed Eleanor Davis, and while you're at it, find out who's been going after Miss Love."

"I thought you said—" Jake couldn't believe his ears.

"I know what I said. Forget that." The chief planted his hat on his head. "Keep me posted."

"Yes, sir."

Jake and the Chief joined the Masters. Samantha and Alan stood, arms wrapped around each other, her eyes swollen from crying. Jake offered her a tissue from a nearby box.

"I'm sorry about your friend," Chief Baker said. "I've assigned Detective Sanders—your brother—to investigate the incident. He'll tell you more about what we discussed later." He tipped his head to her and left.

When he was out of sight, Sam looked at Jake, a question etched between her brows.

"The Chief—"

The door to the emergency room opened. "You can see your friend now."

Jake's mouth went dry. The nurse swiped her ID across a black square on the wall, and a door swung open. They hurried along the wide corridor, dodging beds and hospital personnel hustling from room to room.

He heard Mac's voice before they reached her room.

"Sorry, Doc, but I'm not staying in your hospital tonight."

At the end of the hall, the nurse knocked on a door and

eased it open. Mackenzie sat on the side of the bed, a bandage on her forehead and tousled dark hair framing her face. A man in a white coat sat in a chair facing her. Jake let out the breath he didn't realize he'd been holding in.

"Tell him, Sam. I need to go home." Mac's words crackled with frustration.

Ignoring her, Sam addressed the doctor. "How is she?"

"Your friend was lucky. Minor scratches and bruises. The swelling on her head is reduced. But that's twice in one week." The Doctor raised a hand, forestalling any reply from Mac. "We know from sports that second head injuries can be worse than they appear at first. And that doesn't mean she didn't suffer trauma to her neck or back due to the crash. She needs follow-up scans. I would like her to stay for observation. She insists on leaving."

"I will stay with Miss Love." A woman strode into the room.

"Miss Freebody." The doctor sprang to his feet.

She peered at the doctor's name tag. "You were a good student, and I'm sure you're an adequate doctor. However, I also know that hospitals breed disease." She held out her hand. "Give me a list of your requirements. I'll take excellent care of Miss Love."

The doctor sighed and took out his prescription pad. "Call me if you have any questions or problems."

As the door closed after the doctor, Sam rushed to Mac and pulled her into a big hug. "You scared ten years off my life." She grabbed a handful of her hair. "See all these white hairs?"

"Don't make me laugh." Mac grimaced and wrapped her arms around her waist. "Those are your highlights, goofy."

"Well, I'm sure there's an added wrinkle on my face."

"Don't try to make this all about you." Mac chuckled. "I was the one nearly crushed to death."

"I know." Sam stilled, and tears flooded her blue eyes. She grabbed a tissue.

As Jake and his brother-in-law watched from across the room, there was a look of a deep and abiding love for Samantha on Alan's face. Jake had seen it before but never understood. Why was it so clear to him now?

At some point, Miss P had slipped from the room. She returned with a wheelchair. "Time to—what is it you say, Mrs. Masters?"

"Time to rock and roll." Sam escorted Mac to the chair. "Your chariot awaits, my queen."

"If you bow, I'll run over your toes," Mac growled.

"Now, dear." Miss Freebody propelled her through the door. "We'll have none of that."

"I'll take over, Miss P, while you get your car." Jake maneuvered the chair through the corridor. "Sam, you and Alan should go on home and get some sleep. I've got this."

Outside, Sam leaned over and hugged her friend. "See you tomorrow, girlfriend."

When they were alone, Jake squatted next to Mac's wheelchair. He placed a hand on the arm. Their fingers touched, and warmth spread up his arm. Had she felt it too?

A car pulled into the emergency room pickup area, and Miss Freebody got out. "Let's get you home."

Jake helped her into the front seat. He leaned in to fasten her buckle. Her hair smelled of mint, and he lingered a moment longer.

"Thank you." She touched his hand.

"I'll follow you home to be sure you arrive safely."

He stared at the taillights of Miss P's car ahead. He fought to keep a professional perspective, but his feelings for Mac were making it harder and harder.

The escalation from threats to hit-and-run had him

worried. He knew Mac and Sam wouldn't give up on the case. Like the Chief said, if he were going to keep them safe, he'd have to solve the murder of Eleanor Davis—and fast.

Miss P's large sedan turned into Mac's driveway, but what caught Jake's eye was the dark pickup pulling away from the curb as his cruiser neared the house. He followed it to the end of the block. The big vehicle was nowhere in sight. Where had it gone?

Jake returned to park outside Mac's house, stuffed his hands in his coat pockets, and leaned his head against the seatback. It was going to be a long night.

CHAPTER 21

Mac shuffled down the hall to the rocker by her living room window. A groan escaped her lips as she lowered herself onto the cushioned seat. Every part of her body hurt—even her eyelids.

"This will make you feel better." Miss Freebody handed her a mug of steaming liquid. "Your tea collection is limited, but I found a bag of chamomile, which is good for inflammation."

"Thank you." Mac managed a smile. She'd prefer a cup of black coffee, but she wasn't about to complain. As Mama said, that would be "rude, crude, ill-bred, and socially unacceptable." She took a sip. Hmm. Not bad.

She gazed outside and lowered her mug. Had Jake been there all night? She dug her cell phone out of her robe pocket.

"What's up?"

"Come in and have breakfast. We need to talk."

Jake climbed out of his squad car and stretched. She'd been so angry with him, but after her accident, when she heard his voice at her window ... She drank some more tea.

A knock at the door. Mac looked down at her terrycloth

robe covering her flannel pajamas. And her hair—her fingers worked through tangles and attempted to comb her mane into place.

Miss Freebody hustled to the front door and peered through the peephole. "Detective, come in."

"Morning, Miss P." He glanced at Mac. "And thanks for inviting me for breakfast."

"Of course." Miss Freebody raised an eyebrow in Mac's direction. "It will be ready soon. Why don't you have a seat while Mackenzie gets dressed?"

Taking the hint, Mac rose. Jake was watching, so there could be no shuffling now. She prepared for a struggle to make her gait natural, but there was no need. The pain had subsided —for the most part. Maybe the tea helped after all.

After easing into sweats and brushing her hair, Mac returned to find the other two seated at the table and a steaming plate of eggs and bacon ready for her.

"Delicious." Jake took a sip of orange juice. "As good as Cowan's."

A blush blossomed on Miss Freebody's narrow face and neck. "I doubt that, but you always were a sweet young man, Jake Sanders."

"How are you feeling, Mac?" Jake gave her a look that made her pulse quicken. Was this the look he gave all his girlfriends?

"Better." She tore her gaze from his. "Some bruising." She touched her chest. "Miss P gave me some tea that helped with the aches and pains." She slipped him a quick smile. "Thanks for being there for me. At the crash. I appreciate it."

"My pleasure."

The warmth in his voice washed over her, and she turned to him once more. "Sam told me the Chief was at the hospital last night. What did he want?"

"He ordered me to solve the murder of Eleanor Davis and find out who's been coming after you."

"I wish he'd done that sooner."

"No sense going there." Jake swallowed. "Do any of your neighbors own black trucks?"

"Why?"

He sighed. "Mac, please, just answer the question."

"Fine. I don't remember seeing any around." She caught his gaze. "Why?"

"Last night, as I pulled up, a black pickup took off from down there." He motioned to where he'd seen the truck.

She shivered. Was it the same truck that ran into her? She glanced at Jake.

"Mac, what happened last night? Why were you out without an escort?"

"You tell me. Sam and I saw the officer out front take off in a hurry about four in the afternoon." She smiled at Miss P as the older woman took her dirty plate. "We thought something big must have happened."

"There was a car chase that started in St. Louis County, headed toward Washington. We needed all available patrol cars to assist once they hit Franklin County." Jake scratched where a growth of hair shadowed his chin. "But he should have been back before you left for dinner."

"He wasn't." She moved her shoulders and grimaced. "I need to move to the living room and my rocking chair."

"Sure." Jake offered his arm.

"How would someone know about the car chase and that all available officers were to report?"

"I think I can answer that one," Miss P said. "They possess a police ban radio like mine."

"Sam and I need one of those." Mac made a mental note.

The doorbell rang. Jake motioned the women back and put

his eye to the peephole. "Sam." He opened the door. "It's about time you got here, sis."

"Very funny." She made a beeline for her partner. "How are you?"

"I'm fine. Miss P's taking great care of me. Give me one more day, and I'll be back to normal."

"Good." Sam hung her jacket on a dining room chair. "I'll catch us up on paperwork while you rest."

"I've left some sandwiches for lunch, ladies." Miss P put her purse on her arm. "I will be supervising the work at the office if you need me. Samantha, Mackenzie's medicine is on the counter with instructions. Call if you have any questions."

"Thanks, Miss P."

After Miss Freebody left, Jake sat across from Mac. "Before I leave, did you learn anything useful from Ivy last night?"

Dinner with Ivy seemed like a week ago. "Let me think." She rubbed her forehead. "She confirmed that Rob and Eleanor dated in high school and were rumored to be having an affair recently. But, according to her, it hadn't ended by the time Eleanor died."

"He lied to us and his wife," Sam said.

"There was something else." Mac wrinkled her brow in concentration. She remembered. "Faye was pregnant. She ended up losing the baby."

"Whoa."

"According to Ivy, she blamed her miscarriage on the stress from her husband's affair—or relationship—with Eleanor." Mac paused. "Sam and I were talking about motives. Assuming the guys coming after us are the same ones who killed Eleanor, their motive must be a strong one."

"I think they're hired goons, but you're right." Jake nodded. "Motive is important, and because the attacks keep escalating, I'd say it's money."

"How can that be? Connor would be the obvious suspect. But he was acquitted, and the police didn't find any evidence of him hiring someone to kill his wife." Mac couldn't sit still. She set the rocker in motion. "And like I told Sam, her brothers are out of the picture. They're a very close family. Besides, the boys inherit the business. Not only do they get their share, but the potential to make a whole lot more."

"What are we missing?" Sam said.

"Did I help clear a guilty man? Could Connor be the murderer? But he has an alibi."

"Start with the facts," Jake said. "What else do you have to investigate?"

"Robert Jackson mentioned something about the prenups. I guess we'll start there." Mac stopped rocking. "Would you go visit Mr. Fischer with us?"

"Tomorrow is Sunday. I'll get a meeting set up for Monday or Tuesday. In the meantime, I'll light a fire under Detective Young. See what he's found out," Jake said. "What other suspects did you come up with?"

"Only Robert, with the motive of love, if he and Eleanor were having an affair and she wanted to end it and he didn't, and Faye, out of jealousy and hate."

"You know, Faye Jackson has money of her own. She inherited from her grandfather, part of the Busch family."

"What's your point?"

"If Eleanor threatened to ruin Robert's marriage, he stood to lose a lot."

"So, money could be his motive as well."

"Yes, but Faye knows about him and Eleanor," Sam said.

"She does now. The question is, when did she find out?" Jake glanced out the window. "The shift officer's arrived. I need to go."

He hugged Sam and walked over to Mac. What was he going to do? She tensed.

"I'll come by later to check on you."

"Thanks." She gave him a quick smile. For a moment, she thought he might hug her too. The question was, did she want him to? And the answer was—yes and no. How was that for decisive?

CHAPTER 22

"Speaking of Faye, she's calling right now." Mac pressed the speaker button on her phone. "Mackenzie Love."

"Miss Love. It's urgent that I talk to you. Can you meet me in half an hour?"

Mac looked at Sam, who nodded. "Yes. At my home. We'll see you then."

The line went dead.

For the second time in two days, the sleek car pulled into Mac's driveway. But it was a different woman who emerged from the vehicle. Faye Jackson approached, her platinum hair disheveled and her face gray.

"Mrs. Jackson, what's wrong?" Sam escorted her to a corner of the sofa. "Would you like some water?"

"Yes." The woman slumped against the cushions as if her spine could no longer support her. "I have the second autopsy report on my sister." She extracted two stapled pieces of paper from her purse and handed them to Mac.

Mac scanned the document. "This supports what you

believed all along. A lethal injection of potassium chloride killed your sister." Why was she so upset?

Sam handed her a bottled water, and Faye took a long drink.

"Yes. I should feel triumphant." Tears filled her eyes. "But I don't. It's as if I'm back at the beginning—back when the police came to tell me she died. Only this time, they tell me she's been murdered."

Sam sat next to her and offered her a tissue. "I'm so sorry."

"At least now, the police have to investigate," Mac said.

Faye nodded. "But I don't trust them to do the job right. I want you to investigate it as well."

"Okay." Mac put the papers on the table next to her and picked up her notebook. "We'll need some information. Some of it may be hard for you to talk about."

"Have you got anything stronger than water?" She looked at Sam.

"Iced tea. Coffee. Lemonade," Sam said. "Or soft drinks."

"That's not what I had in mind, but I'll take a coffee if it's okay."

"One coffee, coming up. Mac?"

Mac shook her head. "Faye, Sam and I are equal partners."

The woman gave her a quizzical look. "I'm not sure I know what you mean."

"Sam is kind enough to fetch your drinks and a tissue when you're crying, but she and I are both private investigators. We will both be working on your case."

"Oh." A faint color rose on her neck. "I didn't mean to offend her or you."

"None taken. I wasn't sure you were aware of the facts."

Sam handed her a steaming mug of coffee.

"Thank you, Mrs. Majors. You're very kind."

"My pleasure." Sam smiled sweetly at her and sat next to Mac.

"First, was your sister's marriage a happy one, in your opinion?"

"At first, but after their third child was born, she and her husband seemed distant." Faye stared into her cup. "She told me he could be abusive—not physically, but mentally. I told her to leave him, but she felt the children still needed their father."

"Do you think he was having an affair?"

"I don't think he had time for one. All he did was work."

"What does he do?" Sam leaned forward.

"He owns his own accounting firm. It's not very big, and he does most of the work himself."

"What about Mary Elizabeth? Do you think she might have had a lover?"

"I don't know." Faye breathed a sigh. "I hate to think that of my own sister, but lately, she seemed happy. When I questioned her about it, she'd change the subject. I know she made lots of trips to Kansas City and asked me to cover for her. She told her husband we were going together." She pressed her lips together. "I'm glad I never had to."

"Do you think you could get us her cell phone?" Mac jotted a note on her pad.

"I'm not sure who has it."

"Or, if you can't get it, maybe you can at least see it," Sam said. "Make screenshots of her train tickets and send them to yourself. I'll show you how."

"I'll try. I'm not very good with things like that."

"Anything you can get for us will be a big help."

"What about this potassium chloride injection?" Faye pulled another tissue from the box beside her. "Would M.E. have suffered?"

"No." No sense in adding to the woman's grief, and most likely, it would have been quick. "Since your sister had a heart condition already, the drug would have taken effect almost before she realized what was happening."

"The real question is how did her husband get hold of the drug and, even more important, how did he administer it when he was miles away on a school trip with their son?"

"I don't know, but I'm sure he's behind it." Faye stood. "Please find the answers soon. I'll work on the cell phone."

"Mrs. Jackson, please sit down." Mac waited for her to settle. "Did you kill Eleanor Davis?"

Mac prepared herself for a reaction, but when it came, even Mac was surprised.

"I thought about it." Faye Jackson straightened and gave Mac a steely look. "But I decided she wasn't worth the possible consequences. Nor was my husband."

"Even though you blamed the loss of your baby on her relationship with your husband?"

"I should have known." She gave a bitter laugh. "There are no secrets in a small town. No, not even then. Am I glad she's dead? Yes. But did I kill her? No." She stood again. "Anything else?"

Mac rose. "No, ma'am. We'll get busy on your case—that is, if you still want us to."

"If you're as dogged about Mary Elizabeth's case as you have been about Eleanor's, I have no doubt you will find out who killed both women. That's all that matters."

"Detective Young, come with me." Jake led the way to his office. He eased into his chair and took a sip of his lemonade. "What have you been able to learn?"

"I got the railroad security footage from the day Eleanor Davis left and the day she returned." He extracted his phone from his pocket. "I'll send you my notes. On Thursday, we've got a pretty good shot of her boarding the train with Greg Williams, and it clearly shows his left hand." Young passed his phone to Jake.

"Good." Jake gave the phone back. "What about Saturday —the day she was killed?"

"We see her exit the train, but there's a surprise. A few minutes later, Robert Jackson gets off."

"Jackson? Are you sure?"

"Yes, sir." The Detective scooted his phone across the desk toward Jake. "I worked for Jackson for two summers in high school."

Jake handed Young's phone back. "Anything on the train tickets?"

"I got to thinking that if Mrs. Davis was making as many trips as you say she was, she'd probably have a rail pass." Young swiped to a new screen. "Those allow a person to make multiple trips without—"

"Get to the point, Vic."

"Yes, sir." Young cringed.

Jake ran a hand through his hair. "Sorry. Didn't mean to bark. You're doing a great job."

"Thank you, sir. I know I talk too much." The Detective shifted in his chair. "Anyway, Eleanor *Davis* didn't have a rail pass, but Eleanor *Fischer* did. It seemed she got a new credit card and new phone in her maiden name in order to get the pass."

"Good thinking." Jake smiled at his Detective. "I'm not sure I would have thought to ask about Fischer. What did you find out about her trip history?"

"She returned from K.C. on the Tuesday before her death,

as you thought." He looked at his phone. "And left again Thursday with Greg Williams."

Jake straightened. "Here's what I need you to do next." He tapped the desk between Young and himself. "Find out if Greg Williams had a rail pass, and I guess Robert Jackson while you're at it." He paused. "Search for Mary Elizabeth and her husband, and Connor Davis too. And Faye Jackson. Might as well get them all."

"I wasn't aware we were investigating the Mary Elizabeth case."

"We're not—yet. But I have a feeling we may be."

"Okay." Vic Young shrugged.

"Have you got anything else?"

"The print on the second note isn't in the system, and the Davises' prenups aren't public record."

"What about the truck?"

"The dealer is getting together the names of all the people he's sold black trucks to in the last five years. It seems that the model hasn't changed a lot." Young rubbed his forehead. "I have a feeling it's going to be a very long list."

"One more thing. I want you to put together a photo of Greg Williams with a few options showing him with a beard, gray hair, a hat. You know the drill. Then set up meetings with the victims of the robberies and ask if anyone like that has ever been to their homes."

"Got it."

"First, set a meeting up for Monday or Tuesday with Mr. Fischer. For me. Make it late morning. Can you have the ID kit by then?"

"Sure, if I get on it right away."

"I'm not stopping you." Jake grinned at him. "On second thought. One more thing." Jake jotted a note on his pad, ripped it out, and handed it to Young.

"I found a police scanner app for our phones." Mac glanced at Sam. "I'm sending you the link."

"Does it cost anything?"

"Some, but it's worth it. It's a business expense." Mac tapped her screen. "Let's see how it works."

A notification appeared. Black truck found abandoned off Mission Drive by Dubois Creek.

"Somebody found a black truck." Mac got to her feet. "Come on."

"You're supposed to be taking it easy today, remember?"

"You'll be driving and all I have to do is ride. That's easy." When Mac opened her door, the police officer stood ready to knock.

"Miss Love, we've found the truck."

"We know. We were about to go there."

"Come with me, please."

They traveled along Fifth Street to Old Highway 100. About a mile later, they made a left on Mission Drive, and at the curve where the concrete plant sat, they went straight onto a dirt road. Police cars marked their destination.

"Is my brother here?" Sam said.

"No, ma'am. I think Detective Young is in charge."

Mac shuddered as she caught sight of the large black pickup stuffed in the underbrush. Was this the monster truck that chased her down on Fifth Street and haunted her dreams? She inspected the grill as best she could. Trees and bushes blocked a good portion of it, but she made out scratches and what seemed like paint transfer the color of her car.

"What do you think?" Detective Young said.

"It looks like the truck," Mac said.

"We'll have forensics go over it and see what they can find.

With luck, we'll get the guys." Detective Young put a hand out to stop Mac and Sam from leaving. "Are you going to see Detective Sanders later?"

"I will," Mac said.

"Would you tell him I've got an appointment with Mr. Fischer scheduled for ten-thirty Monday morning at Fischer's office? I tried texting, but the service here is lousy." Young smiled at them. "I'm going to be tied up with this for a while, and I'm afraid I might forget to text him later."

"Sure." Mac shot a look at Sam. Jake wouldn't be the only one meeting with Fischer on Monday morning.

"Hang on." Young pulled two bulletproof vests from his car and handed them to Mac and Sam. "Detective Sanders asked me to get these for you. You're to wear them anytime you leave home."

They gave each other a questioning look and hefted the body armor. Once inside the officer's police car, Mac slipped hers on.

"Ouch." She undid it and rubbed her chest. "It hurts where the airbag bruised me. I don't know if I can wear this thing."

"It doesn't look very comfortable." Sam eyed her vest. "I'll talk to Jake and see how—"

"I can answer that, ma'am," the officer in the driver's seat said. "He's serious."

Mac raised an eyebrow at Sam. "I guess we have an addition to our wardrobes."

When they got back, Jake's car was in the drive. He greeted them as they crossed the street. "Good. You've got your vests."

Both women grunted.

"Mine hurts my bruising." Mac unlocked the door.

"Better that than dead." Jake opened it for her.

"Somehow I knew you'd say that."

"Did you come to make sure we hadn't thrown them out

the window on the way home?" Sam raised an eyebrow at her brother.

"No. I have information to share." Jake wandered into the kitchen. "Can I have some lemonade?"

"I don't know. Can you?" Sam said.

"Hah, hah." Jake grinned at her. "May I have some lemonade?"

"Help yourself."

Once seated at the table, Sam opened her computer. "What did you come to tell us, bro?"

"Detective Young found out a few things."

"Great." Mac pulled her pad and pencil over.

"He got railway footage that confirmed all we talked about. Eleanor left with a man with a missing digit on his left hand. She returned on Saturday, the day she died." He took a sip of his lemonade. "Someone else got off the train that day too. Robert Jackson."

"Jackson?" This case was like a children's game where a player moved forward a few spaces and then slid back five. "I guess another talk with Mr. Jackson is on our list."

"Leave that. You two need to rest." Jake stood. "Tomorrow's Sunday, and I've asked Young to set up a meeting with Mr. Fischer for Monday or Tuesday."

"It's Monday at ten-thirty," Sam said. "We saw him when we went to look at the black truck. He doesn't have good cell service out there."

"Got it." Jake put on his hat.

Sam walked him to the door. "Love you, bro."

"Same here." Jake gave her a quick hug. "Mac." He tipped his hat at Mac.

Her mood plummeted. "I think I need a nap. Why don't you go on home and rest too?"

"Are you sure?"

Mac nodded.

"I could use the rest." Sam hung her vest over her arm. "I won't see you tomorrow. Alan and I are going to St. Louis. But Monday, I'll be here as usual."

"Safe travels."

Mac watched her friend drive away. Intending to spread out on her bed for a nap, she walked into her bedroom, but when she came through the door, she knew what she needed. Her chair beckoned with her Bible open on the table beside it.

"I need a word from You, Lord. I'm feeling bummed." Mac sat and picked up her Bible. Her eyes landed on chapter five, verse seven of First Peter.

"Give all your worries and cares to God, for he cares about you."

Her mouth curved into a smile. Mama always said, *"Tell Jesus. He'll know what to do."*

It was taking her a while to learn that lesson, but maybe it was finally sinking in. She closed her Bible and lowered her head in prayer.

After several minutes, Mac opened her eyes. There was one more thing she needed to take care of before she ate. She needed a car to drive. She keyed in rental agencies on her computer. The one in Washington offered a discount on a compact sedan that looked a lot like her old car. They would deliver to her house too. Perfect.

CHAPTER 23

Mac sang along with the worship music on her radio as she prepared breakfast. She glanced at the clock. Plenty of time for a shower.

Mac slipped into her dress slacks and linen blouse. She appreciated Jake's concern for her safety, but the bulletproof vest hurt her bruised chest. Besides, somehow it didn't seem right to wear it to church. Grabbing her purse on the way out, she waved to the officer on duty as she got into her rental car.

When they arrived, the uniformed police officer escorted her from her car to the sanctuary. Mac took a seat a few rows from the back and tried to ignore the questioning stares.

Other worshipers filled the pew where Jake, Sam, and Alan usually sat. Sam and Alan were visiting his grandparents in St. Louis, and Jake was on duty. She missed her friends.

Dear Lord, help me focus on worshiping You.

Organ music filled the air with one of her favorite hymns, and the choir director motioned for them to stand.

After a couple of songs, announcements, and the children's message, Mac settled in to listen to today's sermon. The topic centered on Ephesians, chapter six, and the armor of God. When the pastor read verse thirteen, "Therefore, put on every piece of God's armor so you will be able to resist the enemy in the time of evil," Mac's pulse quickened. She thought of her vest at home on the bed.

"Okay, Lord, I get it," she whispered.

After leaving church, she drove by the office to inspect the progress. New windows, new siding, and patched holes healed the ugly scar on their little house and on her heart. Sunshine broke through the patchy clouds and lit up the front porch.

"A little paint, and we'll be back in business." The corners of her mouth lifted in a smile, reflecting the hope lifting her spirits. Maybe they'd solve this case after all.

AFTER A RELAXING SUNDAY, Mac looked forward to their Monday morning meeting with Peter Fischer. Mac and Sam arrived outside Fischer Industries a little before Jake and Detective Young. They pulled into the lot across from the buff brick building and parked.

"Did you spot the dark blue van in the employee's parking lot?" Mac said.

Sam nodded. She climbed out and adjusted her blouse. "This vest is so uncomfortable, and it's ruining my figure."

"I get it, but think of it as part of the armor of God."

"If God made it, it would fit better." Sam grimaced.

The unmarked sedan swung into a space two down from them. Detective Young got out and waited for Jake.

Mac caught up to him. "See the dark blue van in the employee lot?"

"Yes." Jake opened the door to the building. "Think it was the one following you?"

"Could be."

Mr. Fischer's assistant waited in the foyer. "This way, ladies and gentlemen." She led the way upstairs and through the building to a corner room with a gleaming conference table. Water and light snacks were placed around the table.

"My goodness, I had no idea I would be so outnumbered." Mr. Fischer laughed as he entered the room. "Maybe I should call in a few of my staff to even the odds."

"That won't be necessary." Jake smiled at him. "Detective Young and I are here merely to ask you some questions regarding the burglary at your home." Jake inclined his head at Mac and Sam. "Miss Love and Mrs. Masters are investigating the death of your daughter and asked if they might take the opportunity to speak with you as well. You being a busy man, I thought you'd rather get this all over with in one meeting rather than two."

"You're correct, Detective. Where do you want to start?"

"We have an ID kit that we'd like you to look at."

Detective Young extracted the sheet of photos from his file and placed it on the table in front of Mr. Fischer. "Do any of these men look familiar to you?"

Fischer drew the paper closer and examined it. "Yes." He nodded. "This one, the man with the gray beard. He worked on my machinery several times." Fischer slid the paper back to Young. "In fact, I believe we had him to the house for dinner once. Very intelligent and interested in all sorts of things." The corners of Fischer's mouth turned down. "Is he the one who robbed me?"

"We think so."

"Have you caught him? Have you recovered my piece?"

"We have him in custody, but no, we haven't found your Micklenburg egg yet. At this stage, we're building our case,"

Jake said. "He was wearing a disguise when he met with you. The next step is for you to come to the station for a line-up."

"Any time." Mr. Fischer turned to Mac and Sam. "Now, young ladies, it's your turn. I know who you are—you got my son-in-law acquitted."

Mac studied Fischer's face. Was he mad about it or okay with it? Connor still worked for him, so ... "Yes, sir. And since we played a part in exonerating the only suspect, we felt it was our duty to find the actual killer."

"Miss Love, I'm well aware of how most of the town feels and the pressure you must be under to exonerate yourself."

Heat rose from her neck to her face. "True, but now it's become more than that."

"I know about the threats and the accident too. As well as the fact that you almost got run over in Kansas City."

Mac stared at him. "How do you know all that?"

Fischer folded his hands on the table. "May I tell you a story?"

She nodded.

"I bought a company in Kansas City, and when Eleanor and Connor first married, I sent him to run it. After three years, Eleanor begged me to create a position for Connor here." He rubbed his thumbs together. "She told me she was homesick, but I found out that Connor was drinking and gambling. I got them back here as fast as I could."

Fischer sighed. "But nothing changed, and finally, Eleanor and Connor separated. When they did, she distanced herself from me." He looked up. "So, I did what I thought best. I hired a private detective out of St. Louis. He tailed her almost everywhere she went and reported back to me." He held up a hand. "Before you ask, the day she was killed, he was conveniently off duty. It seems somebody else knew about him. I don't know who."

"Why didn't you give all this information to the police?" Jake said.

"There was nothing to tell."

"Not even about her meetings with Robert Jackson? Or her trips to the lawyer in Kansas City?"

"And what about the prenups?" Mac said.

"What meetings? What lawyer?" Fischer's face reddened. "And what do her prenups have to do with anything?"

Mac looked first at Jake and then at Sam. What was happening here?

"Who recommended the St. Louis private investigator to you, sir?" Mac bent toward him.

"A woman who was my assistant at one time and is now my friend. Faye Jackson."

Mac wanted to pace, but she couldn't. Her leg bounced under the table—until Sam bumped it with her knee. She uncapped a water bottle and took a swig.

"May we talk about the prenuptial agreement?" Sam smiled at Mr. Fischer.

"I suppose." He leaned back. "What do you want to know?"

"Is there any clause in there about conditions for inheritance on Connor's part in the event Eleanor passes away before he does?"

"The only clause has to do with divorce. If Eleanor and Connor divorced, or were in the process of divorcing, or if she served Connor papers with intent to divorce him—even if he hadn't signed them—then he would not be eligible to inherit her part of my money."

"Do you know if that happened?"

"As far as I know, they were working on getting back together. At least, that's what Connor said. The boy still loved her. I could see that." Deep furrows creased Fischer's brow. "But what's this about an affair and a lawyer in Kansas City?"

"We have evidence that Eleanor made frequent trips to Kansas City to see a lawyer about getting a divorce," Jake said. "As for the affair, that's not for certain. I'm sorry. I think your private investigator wasn't giving you the full story."

"I hope my newest investigator has been." Fischer stared at Mac. "I've had one of my employees tailing you, Miss Love, ever since I heard you were investigating Eleanor's murder. He almost blew his cover the other day."

"The dark blue van? Was that the vehicle that followed me home after dinner at Cowans?" Mac gave him quick smile. "I saw it in your employee parking lot when we came in. Mr. Fischer, if you want to know what we learn, we'll be glad to give you updates. You don't have to waste your employee's time tailing me around."

"I'd like that. I'll pay you, of course."

"However, I need to speak with him," Jake said. "He may have seen something useful."

"I'll call him in here after we're finished."

"Mr. Fischer, did Eleanor use a local law firm to draw up her prenups?"

"Yes. I'll give you their information along with a letter allowing you access to her files." He pressed a button on the table. "This is most disturbing."

"But you don't know who she might have used in Kansas City?"

He shook his head. "I knew she was unhappy, but I had no idea she wanted a divorce. As I said, I thought she and Connor were working on getting back together." He ran a shaky hand across his brow. "Or I wouldn't have kept him on after my daughter's death. I have some decisions to make."

"Mr. Fischer, please do nothing. Remember, we still need to confirm that Eleanor was seeing someone about a divorce. You don't want to upset your organization unless it's necessary," Sam said.

"Very wise, young lady. I'll wait until I hear from you."

Fischer's assistant opened the door, and Mr. Fischer visibly pulled himself together to become the confident owner of a lucrative business once more.

"Would you ask Evans to step in here? And get me the file on Eleanor's prenuptial agreement. It will be in my office desk drawer. Here's the key. Thank you." He looked at his guests. "Is there anything else I can do for you?"

"I don't think so." Jake shifted in his chair.

"When you're through interviewing Evans, he'll see you out." Fischer rose. "Thank you, officers, for your hard work to keep our town safe. Ladies, keep me posted as to your progress."

As Fischer reached for the door, it opened, and his assistant stepped in.

"Here's the file you requested, sir." She handed her boss a folder and his keys. "Mr. Evans didn't show up for work today."

"What do you mean? His van is in the lot. Did you talk to his supervisor?"

"He hasn't seen him all day."

Jake jumped to his feet. "We need to search the building. Is there anywhere you can go that's secure?"

"We have a tornado shelter."

"Does it lock from the inside?" Jake crossed to Fischer's side.

"Yes, but—"

"Please go there now. Along with your assistant. Stay there until I come get you." He peered at Mac and Sam. Should he send them too?

"Don't even think about it," Sam said. "We're trained professionals and can help search."

But could he keep them safe? His stomach knotted.

"Are you wearing your vests?"

They nodded.

"Are you armed?"

More nods.

Sweat trickled down his back. "Stay behind Detective Young."

Jake led the way down the stairs to the first floor. Instead of turning left toward the front door, he went right into the factory. They hastened along an aisle flanked by large machines. The noise vibrated in his chest.

Employees stopped what they were doing and gazed at the small troop of armed men and women passing through. At the end of the long room, a door opened onto a grassy area between the building and the employee parking lot.

Jake slipped through, motioning for the rest of them to wait. He scanned the area.

"Clear. Young, tell the workers to stay away from the door."

After following orders, Young, Mac, and Sam joined Jake outside.

"We're going to check out the van." Jake nodded in the direction they would be going. "Stay alert."

They crossed the grass and approached the vehicle. Jake scanned the trees beyond the lot. Was that a shadow? The hair on the back of his neck stood up. "Down."

A shot echoed off the building. Jake pivoted toward the other three in time to see Sam fall. Her arms flung out as she crashed to the ground.

He raced to her side, but as he reached her, a searing pain hit his leg and he, too, landed in the dirt. He'd been shot. Frustration and anger seared through him. He rolled behind a car close by.

"Jake, are you hurt?" Detective Young said.

"A through and through. You and Mac?"

"Okay. I called for backup. What about Sam?"

"She needs help. She's been shot." The pain in his leg paled next to the pain in his heart. He prayed Sam would live.

"Where's the shooter?"

"In the trees. Not sure where." Jake pushed to a sitting position and struggled out of his shirt. His T-shirt would make good tourniquet strips. With any luck, the shooter may have left by now.

Two squad cars screamed into the lot, spewing officers with guns drawn. A shot slammed into the hood of the first car.

Jake finished tying the strips around his leg and pushed up to peer over the car he hid behind. Where was he? Something moved behind a pine tree. Jake steadied his gun on the hood.

Pine bark exploded where he spotted the shadow. He waited. No return shots. The shooter was finally gone. Jake collapsed to the ground. He didn't have the energy to help Sam.

Lord, take care of my sister.

CHAPTER 24

J ake lay on the gurney and gazed at the dark clouds scudding across the sky. He covered his eyes with his arm. All he saw was his kid sister on the ground. Some protector he was.

Mac placed a hand on his arm. "I'll see you at the hospital."

"No. Take care of Sam. I'm fine." The sensation of her hand burned into his soul.

What if the shooter killed Sam? And Mac? He failed to keep the two most important women in his life safe.

"We're ready if you are, Detective." The EMTs took positions on either side of the gurney.

Jake welcomed the jolt of pain as they lifted him into the ambulance. He deserved it. One tech eased his arm to his side and strapped him in.

"This shouldn't be too bad, but we're going to give you a shot for pain, anyway."

He felt a prick, and warmth spread from his arm through his chest and down his legs. After fighting sleep for a while, he forgot why, and gave in to it.

At the hospital, he woke in a fog as they unloaded him from the ambulance. Certain things registered. The swoosh of the emergency room doors, bright lights flashing by overhead, the chatter of voices. What had they given him?

"He's having a reaction to the painkiller."

Hands moving his legs and arms. Why couldn't he move them himself?

"Get him into a room now."

"His pulse is low."

A tightness on his right arm. Beeping.

Running feet. Urgent voices.

What was happening?

A jab.

Ouch. Good night.

JAKE STRUGGLED to open his eyes. Parts of him ached, while other parts were numb. He swiveled his head on his pillow. Mac's head of dark hair lay near his right hand. He moved his fingers. She stirred and turned to face him.

"You're awake." She raised her head and smiled.

He returned her smile. At least, he thought he did. The numbness covered parts of his face. He flexed his cheeks. That was better.

Mac laughed. "What are you doing?"

Could he talk? He swallowed hard. "Sam?" Not bad.

"What?" She gave him a questioning look.

He'd try again. "Samm."

"Got it. She's okay. A couple of cracked ribs." Mac put her fingers to her lips. "Are you numb?"

He nodded.

"Well, you have been asleep in one position for almost

twelve hours." She motioned to the clock. "You gave me a scare, Jake Sanders. Apparently, you're allergic to codeine."

Rather than talk, he transmitted his question with his eyes.

"The EMTs gave you a painkiller, and you had a reaction." Mac touched his hand. "The docs gave you something to counteract the effects of the drug, and you've slept like a baby through lots of poking and prodding."

Jake touched his outer left leg where he'd been shot and looked at her.

"They sewed you up while you slept. You didn't flinch." She smiled again. "Do you want anything?"

He wanted to get dressed and leave, but that wasn't going to happen soon. He mimicked drinking.

Mac held a cup with a straw to his lips. He managed to get some water without too much dribble. She plucked a tissue from the box and drew it carefully across his chin.

He raised his hand to hers. "Thank you." That was better.

"You're welcome."

The door opened to several voices talking at once.

"You're awake." Sam appeared, holding onto Alan's arm.

The sight of his sister's heart-shaped face and the sound of her voice warmed his heart. *Thank You, Jesus.*

Alan helped his wife into a chair by the bed. "Good to see you, man. You had us worried for a minute."

He swallowed. "That's what Mac's been telling me. I'm ..." He blinked and turned away.

"Hey." Alan laid a hand on his shoulder. "I get it."

"I'm sorry. I failed you guys." Jake forced himself to look each of them in the eye.

"What are you talking about, man?"

"That's silly." Sam gave him a crooked smile.

He looked at Mac.

"You're right." She shrugged. "You're like the rest of us—

weak, imperfect, subject to failure. But we don't expect you to be perfect." She placed a finger on his chest. "You're the only one who expects perfection, and it's about time you cut yourself a break."

"But you and Sam—"

"Are adult women who make our own decisions and take responsibility for our own safety. We don't expect you to keep us free from harm any more than you should expect us to keep you fed."

Alan shrugged a shoulder. "You might as well give it up, Jake. There's no winning with these two."

"Ahem." Miss P stepped close to his bed. "I'm glad to see you're recovering, Detective. And, as for what Miss Love said, she's correct. The true failure is the one who falls and doesn't get up to try again. You are not one of those."

"Thank you." He reached for a tissue and blew his nose. "If I'm going to try again, first I need you to take me home."

"Not quite, Detective Sanders." The doctor glided into the room and motioned everyone away from the bed. "We're going to have the pleasure of your company for one more day. I want to make sure the effects of the narcotic are out of your system and see how your wound is healing." He lifted the covers and exposed Jake's leg. "When you're released, you'll need someone to help change the dressing for a few days, and no driving."

"I'm a police officer. How do you expect me to do my job without driving?"

"That's for you to figure out. I'm in charge of your body." The doctor made some notes on his chart.

Another boss to please? Maybe he should call the Chief and have him talk to the doctor. Could be interesting. He grinned inwardly at the thought.

"If you wish, I can have a word with Chief Baker. He's my

brother-in-law." The doctor smiled at Jake. "They're coming for Sunday dinner."

He should have guessed. Small towns. The grin faded. "Bye, doc."

"Don't worry. You can stay with us for a while." Sam glanced at Alan, who nodded agreement.

The spare bedroom with flower wallpaper, bedspread, and curtains? "I'm not—"

"I'll be glad to come over and take care of you and Sam while Alan is at work." Miss P folded her hands in her lap.

All day with Miss P? "Wait a minute—"

"The only problem is your roommate," Sam said.

"Roommate?" Mac eased her hand away from Jake's.

He'd forgotten about Duke.

"Our dog and your cat do not mix well." Sam looked at Mac with a twinkle in her eye.

"A cat." Mac gave Sam *The Look*.

"Do I get a say in this?" Jake said in a loud voice.

Four expectant faces turned to face him. What did he want? Everything they said made sense. Sam and Alan were family. Miss P was an excellent cook, and she wouldn't pester him. Except —

"None of you are safe until we catch the man who attacked us today. Including you, Alan, and you, Miss P."

CHAPTER 25

J ake was right. "I got this text right before we went outside. It was so noisy in the factory I didn't hear it chime." Mac showed her phone to the others.

I TOLD YOU TO STOP

"Maybe we should quit investigating Eleanor's murder. It's too risky." Mac stared at the message on her phone. "When it was threats against me, it was one thing, but now ..."

Jake shook his head. "This guy has crossed a line. Regardless of whether you continue, I need to find him, and he will not like it."

Miss P raised her hand. "Detective, I believe I have the solution to one of our problems. My late husband and I bought a lovely large home, thinking we would fill it with sons and daughters." She sniffed. "The children never came, but we remained in our home anyway. It has plenty of room for all of us to live there together while you and Samantha heal and we discover who is threatening our friends. What do you say?"

"Where's your house?"

"At the end of Main Street."

"I will give you the downstairs bedroom, Detective, and temporarily move upstairs." She looked over her glasses at the others. "Well?"

"Thanks, Miss P, but I think Alan and I will stay in our own home." Sam reached for her husband's hand. "But it's a good idea for Jake to come stay with you so you can give him the care he needs."

"The Chief told me he's cutting the detail on Mac's house back to daytime only." Jake struggled to sit at a better angle.

"Let me." Alan fiddled with the controls on the side of the bed. "Is that better?"

Jake nodded. "Thanks." He paused to catch his breath. "I can't ask for police officers to watch your house, Sam."

"We don't need any, bro. We'll be careful."

Jake focused on Mac. "What about you? Will you move to Miss P's until we catch these guys?"

"You're saying I'll be on my own at night?"

"Yes. You can still use your house for work during the day."

Mac pinched the bridge of her nose. "I guess I have no choice."

"One more thing. Who gets Duke?"

"He's welcome as well." Miss P nodded. "I will keep Cupric in my bedroom."

"Cupric?"

"My parakeet. He's named after the beautiful blue-green color of copper solutions." Miss P straightened her spine. "We cannot let these hooligans scare us into compliance. As the Detective said, they've gone too far. And I see their heightened threats as confirmation that we're making progress. We must continue."

"Then I guess that's settled. We keep searching for who

killed Eleanor Davis." Mac scanned the faces of her friends. "Which one of us goes and gets the cat?"

They all looked at Mac.

"Thanks for coming with me, Detective Young." Mac took a tentative step inside Jake's house and felt for a light switch. She surveyed the polished wood floors and warm colors of the neat living room. Not what she had expected.

"I'll get the cage." Detective Young turned down a hallway. "Jake said it would be in a closet in the second bedroom."

"Okay." Mac walked into the kitchen and opened the cupboard. She found a can of cat food, an opener, and a dishtowel. Before she could get the can fully opened, the cat was rubbing against her legs. She scooped the stinky contents into a bowl and placed it on the mat.

"Here he is." Mac squatted beside the silky gray animal. "Aren't you handsome? I'm Mac. Has Jake talked to you about me?"

Duke stopped eating and looked at Mac through narrowed green eyes.

Was that cat glaring at her?

"We're taking you to be with Jake." Mac reached a hand to stroke the silky fur.

"*Hissss*." Duke's paw batted her hand away.

"Sorry. Didn't mean to bother you while you're eating." Mac stood. "You're not going to like this either." She dropped the dishtowel over Duke and tucked the struggling feline against her body. "This is going to hurt me more than it hurts you," she murmured.

And she was right.

Young rushed in with the carrier and Mac wrangled the

squirming mass of fur and claws inside. When Duke settled down, she slid the half-eaten can of food inside the cage, and pressed a tissue on her thumb where Duke scratched her through the towel.

"That wasn't too bad," Detective Young said.

Mac glared at him.

AT MISS FREEBODY'S DOOR, Mac waved to the officer and carried the small animal cage inside. "I'll get my bags in a moment. Where would you like me to put Duke?"

"You can release him in here." The elderly lady waved a graceful arm around her elegant foyer.

"Are you sure?"

"My dear, they're only things."

"Okay." Mac glared through the opening at the green eyes. "Don't mess things up. Okay?"

"*Mrawr.*"

She placed the carrier on the floor and opened the door. Instead of streaking out of the cage, the gray cat stepped through the opening, head high. Once fully out, he sat, front legs together, tail wrapped tightly against his body, and surveyed his surroundings.

"My, aren't you a fine specimen?" Miss Freebody ran a hand down his back. "What a beautiful shade of gray, and those black stripes."

"That he is." Mac gave a brief laugh. "I'm still amazed that he's Jake's cat." She pushed herself upright. "I'll get my things."

"And I will fix us some dinner."

Mac pulled her suitcases from the trunk and set them on the drive. Built in 1838 on a bluff overlooking the Missouri

River, the elegant two-story house sat in the middle of about one and a half acres at the end of Main Street. Trees and shrubbery shielded the house from casual spying.

And yet, as Mac closed her trunk, she felt as if someone watched her every move. A rustle sounded in the shrubbery by the gate. She stopped, straining to see into the darkness. A breeze brushed cobwebs across her face. She swept them away, picked up her luggage, and ran for the house.

After locking the outside door behind her, Mac followed Miss P upstairs to her bedroom. A rocker stood by the window, and as soon as Miss P left, Mac eased herself into the chair and closed her eyes. Had there been someone out there? Or was her anxiety getting the best of her?

Duke landed in her lap, leaned against her chest, and placed a gentle paw on her arm.

"*Mrawr.*"

"Now you want to be friends, do you? After you drew first blood?" Mac gave a low chuckle. "I can see why Jake loves you." She ran her hand over his gleaming coat. "But I need to go to bed." She stood, lifting him off her lap. "Good night, my friend."

Mac hit the *STOP* button on her phone alarm. Seven a.m. Hazy light shone in around the drawn shades. She stared at the antique lamp on the table next to her. Where was she? Maybe she'd been hit on the head too many times.

She bolted upright, swung her legs out of bed, and crossed to the window. A beautiful expanse of lawn arced down to the railroad tracks with the river beyond. A gray cat with black stripes pushed the door open and ambled into the bedroom.

"Duke." Mac picked him up and was rewarded by a head

nuzzle under her chin. "Now I remember." She also remembered why she set her alarm. "Got to move. Sorry." Mac placed her furry friend on the floor and headed for the bathroom.

When she was dressed, Mac realized she didn't know how to get back to where her car was parked. After one wrong turn, she entered the kitchen. "I guess I didn't pay enough attention last night, Miss P. If it weren't for the delicious aroma, I'm not sure I could have found my way here from the bedroom."

"It can be confusing. There have been several additions to the house since it was built." She scooped two omelets onto plates and carried them to the kitchen table. "Did you sleep well?"

"Yes, thank you." Mac poured herself a cup of coffee. "You have a beautiful home. I had no idea you were married."

"Yes." A soft smile played on the lips of the older woman. "For forty years before he passed away. Ten years ago next month. I preferred to use my maiden name as a teacher."

"I'm sure he was a wonderful man."

"He was." Miss Freebody peered at Mac. "Eat before it gets cold."

Mac took a bite of her omelet. "This is fantastic. What time is it?"

"Eight-thirty." Miss Freebody smiled at her.

"Yikes. I need to get moving. I'm supposed to meet Sam at the hospital at ten." She took another bite. "I may be late."

"You've got time." Miss P picked up her fork. "I'll be at the office supervising the painters if you need me." She motioned to Mac's plate and mug. "Don't worry about those. I'll take care of them."

"Thanks." Mac grabbed her jacket and purse and scurried out the door.

At the hospital, Mac and Sam flanked Jake's bed. He gazed at them with clear eyes, and his skin color was back to normal.

"When are they letting you out of here?" Mac flashed him a smile.

"As soon as the doc sees me, and they fit me for crutches. The nurse said my blood tests and my wound look good."

"That's great." Sam squeezed his hand.

"How are you, sis?"

"Hurting. It's going to take a while for my cracked ribs to heal, but it could be worse. If you hadn't insisted on these vests, I wouldn't be here." She gave him a tremulous smile. "Thanks, bro."

A tinge of jealousy zipped through Mac. She loved her sisters, but she'd always wanted a brother too. Was that part of her attraction to Jake? Best not to try to unravel those feelings now. They had a case to solve.

"Do you think that was a hired shooter?"

"Not sure." Jake's deep blue eyes darkened in thought. "Most everyone around here has a gun and is a pretty good shot."

"Even Faye?"

He gave a sharp laugh. "I've seen that woman place five rounds in the middle of a target at fifteen yards. She used to practice at the same gun range I used."

"That's good," Sam said.

"Real good."

"So, we can't rule anyone out yet. It could be Roger or Faye … or Connor." Mac sighed. "I have this terrible feeling that I've messed up big time. I think I need to go back over some things."

"Like what?"

"For one, Connor's alibi. I think I may take Dr. David Ulrich up on his invitation to dinner."

"Why?" Jake gave her a sharp look.

"Something tells me he's the key to this whole thing." A text dinged on Mac's phone. "Miss P wants us to swing by the office to inspect the work. I can go by myself, Sam, if your ribs are hurting."

"I'm fine. I'll let Alan know he doesn't have to pick me up." She stood and winced. "These vests aren't kind to cracked ribs."

"Better a little pain than—"

"The alternative." Sam rolled her eyes. "I know, bro, and I agree. I'm just not good at the whole suffering in silence thing."

He snorted. "Don't I know it."

"We'll talk to you later at Miss P's." Mac stopped. "Wait. How will you get there?"

"Detective Young is taking me over once I'm released from here." He raised a hand. "But, Mac, I don't want you confronting Ulrich on your own. Don't do anything until we talk some more."

Irritation and anger flashed through her. She pressed her lips together to keep from saying something she'd later regret. A thumbs up and she was out the door.

CHAPTER 26

"Thanks for the ride, Detective." Jake opened the door and maneuvered his crutches onto the pavement outside Miss Freebody's home.

"No problem." Detective Vic Young offered his arms for support. "I've got a few things to report if you feel up to it."

"Sure. Help me inside, and we'll find a place to sit." Jake leaned against the squad car. It'd been a long time since he'd navigated on crutches.

"Let me get your bag from the trunk and see if Miss Freebody is home."

"Detective Young." The door opened before he could knock. "I'll take that while you help Detective Sanders inside."

"Why don't you two sit at the kitchen table while I put your luggage in your bedroom?" Miss Freebody hurried up a short flight of stairs off the breakfast room. When she returned, she eyed his crutches. "I do hope you can make it up those few steps. If not, I can make up a bed for you in the den on the couch."

"I'll be fine, Miss P." Jake felt better already. Her warm

kitchen, with its relaxing view of spacious green grass and blue sky, soothed his aching body and spirit.

"*Mrawr*." Duke ran into the room and leaped into Jake's lap.

"Good to see you, too, buddy." He held the cat against his chest and stroked its back. "Have you been good?"

"He's a most pleasant house guest." Miss P opened her refrigerator. "How about something to eat and drink?" After placing a plate of crackers and cheese on the table, along with frosty glasses of lemonade, Miss P retired to the den.

Jake took a sip of his lemonade. "What's up, Vic?"

"First, the shooter got away. We canvased the area to see if anybody noticed anyone or anything, but no luck."

"Keep me in the loop on that." Jake eased himself into another position. He was tired and his leg ached. "What did they find at the scene? Anything?"

"Some nine-millimeter shell casings by the pine tree and a footprint." Young paused. "We found Evans. With his throat slit."

"I was afraid of that." Jake ran a hand down his face. "Where was he?"

"Stuffed in a garbage bag out back of the factory. If you hadn't started the search yesterday, we would have missed him. The trash was due to be picked up today."

"Were you able to get the reports he made to Fischer?"

"More bad news. The file's missing."

"Somebody on the inside of Fischer's company is part of this." Jake clenched his jaw. What a time to be injured. "Any usable forensics from Evan's van?"

Young shook his head.

"Of course not." Jake pinched the bridge of his nose. "What else?"

"I checked on railway passes for Greg Williams, Robert

Jackson, Mary Elizabeth, her husband, and Connor Davis." Young pulled his phone from his pocket. "Everyone had a pass except Mary Elizabeth's husband. And, oddly enough, Connor Davis did the same thing Eleanor did. He took out a new credit card and got a burner phone to get his pass."

"That is strange." Jake stared out the window. "When was the last trip listed on his pass?"

"I thought you'd never ask." Young held his phone so Jake could read it.

The day Eleanor was killed. A chill ran down his spine.

He took the phone from his Detective and peered more closely at where Connor got on the train and where he departed. Hermann to Kirkwood. Not Washington.

"I'm getting frustrated now. This goes beyond strange." Jake handed Young his phone. "Have you talked to Robert Jackson about why he was on the train?"

"No, sir." Young made a note.

"What about interviews with other robbery victims?"

"That's the only good news. So far, they all recognize our man, Greg Williams, in one shape or another."

"Have you kept the Chief up to date on all this?"

"Yes, sir."

"Good work, Detective." He reached for a cracker and cheese slice. "We know about the prenups. I assume you have that folder from Fischer."

"Yes, sir."

"We need to contact the lawyer who drew them up. And last is the truck. Any luck discovering who purchased it?"

"Not yet, but now that we have the VIN, it should be easy."

"Maybe. Nothing's been easy in this case so far."

"Detective Young," Miss P entered the kitchen. "It's time for me to change the detective's dressing on his wound. Would you help him into his bedroom, please?"

"Sure." Young gave Jake a questioning look. "How's she going to ... you know."

"I've got a pair of shorts on under my pants."

"Good thinking." Young supported Jake as he hobbled across the floor.

His injury throbbed with every step, but he refused to give in to the pain. The few stairs up to his bedroom turned out to be easier than he thought they'd be. The space was narrow enough to grab the railing on one side and place his other hand on the wall.

"Thanks, Vic. I'll take it from here. You might as well go on. I think I'll rest for a while after Miss P changes my bandage."

"WHAT DO YOU THINK?" Mac couldn't keep from smiling. Their office building looked good. Better than good—it looked great.

"I love it." Sam did a slow turn, her face reflecting pure joy. "The pale blue color is perfect."

"I think so too." Mac ran her hand over the back wall. "You can't tell where any of the holes were." *Thank You, Jesus.*

"When do you want to move back in?"

"Whenever you're ready."

"Tomorrow." Sam clapped her hands. "I can't wait."

"Great, but you know what that means, right?" Mac gave her an evil grin. "We need to go grocery shopping."

"Suddenly my head hurts." Sam placed the back of her hand on her forehead and closed her eyes.

"I'm not buying it, partner. Get in the car." Mac's cell phone rang. Detective Young? Her stomach churned. "What's happened? Is Jake okay?"

"Detective Sanders is fine. He's resting."

"Thank God." Mac gave Sam a thumbs up. "What do you

need?"

"Nothing. Robert Jackson is coming into the station for an interview. I thought you might want to be there."

"Does the Chief know you're inviting us?"

"It was his idea."

Mac's mouth dropped open.

"Hello?"

Sam took the phone. "Yes, Detective, we'll be there. What time?"

"Three o'clock. I'll meet you at the desk."

"See you then." Sam handed the phone back to Mac and laughed. "Close your mouth, dear. It's very unbecoming."

"Ha, ha." Mac narrowed her eyes at Sam. "That gives us just enough time to shop and have a bite of lunch."

Sam sighed.

MAC SLOWED as they walked toward the glass doors of the Public Safety Building. Detective Young stood outside, pants starched, legs slightly apart, hands clasped in front of him. The sight of him made her miss Jake.

"Are you okay?" Sam touched her arm.

"This case makes my head hurt. Figuratively and literally. I'll be glad when we solve it."

"You and me both. So, let's rock and roll."

"Ladies, I'm glad you could come." Detective Young opened the door for them. "I need your help. You know more about the case than I do."

"Will you be interviewing Robert Jackson?"

"Yes, along with Detective Sergeant Hoover. But we're going to give you mics so you can prompt us on questions you think we should be asking."

"Great." Mac's pulse quickened.

As they entered the squad room, Sam nudged her. "This is exciting." Her blue eyes sparkled.

Mac grinned at her. They sat before the monitors and listened to the technician.

The young man pushed some keys and handed them earpieces with mics. "When you want to talk, press here. I suggest you speak low. If they can't hear you, they'll let you know. Okay?"

Mac and Sam nodded.

The screen came to life with a picture of a room. One chair faced the camera, and two sat with their backs to it. Detective Young entered and faced the camera. "Miss Love, say something so I can check your mic."

"Can you hear me?" Mac spoke in a whisper.

"A little louder."

Mac tried again, and Young gave the okay sign. He went through the same process with Sam. Detective Sergeant Hoover entered and nodded at the camera. Young left and returned with Robert Jackson.

"Would you like something to drink, Mr. Jackson?" Detective Young paused before taking his seat.

"No, thank you." Robert sat back and crossed his legs.

Mac leaned closer to her screen. Was he as at ease as he seemed?

"Do you know why we called you in today?" Detective Sergeant Hoover looked up from his notebook.

"I can guess."

"What would you guess?"

"That it has to do with Eleanor Davis."

"Why would we want to talk to you about Eleanor Davis?"

Robert Jackson planted his feet on the floor and faced the police officers. "Come on, guys. I heard the rumors going around about Eleanor and me. That we were having some torrid love affair."

Mac pressed a button, and the camera zoomed in on Robert. A sheen of sweat appeared on his forehead.

"Were you?" Detective Young cocked his head to one side.

"No. Eleanor and I were friends."

"Ask him if Faye, his wife, knew about him and Eleanor," Mac said.

"Did your wife know about your friendship with Mrs. Davis?" Young emphasized the word friendship.

"Of course she did."

"Before she died or after?" Mac spoke into the mic.

"Before she died or after?"

Robert Jackson narrowed his eyes. "I had nothing to do with Eleanor's death. We were friends. She came to me for advice about her marriage."

"That isn't what I asked."

Jackson bent forward and clasped his hands. "After."

"How did your wife take it?" Detective Young shifted in his chair.

Mac looked at Sam. Her face was filled with sorrow. She was so soft-hearted.

"Are you sure you want to watch this?" Mac touched her arm.

She nodded. "I'll be okay."

"She was hurt and mad at first. But I told her I'd stopped meeting with Eleanor. She believed me—that my relationship with Eleanor was only a friendship and that I was committed to her and our marriage. She forgave me."

"Wow. She's quite a woman. I'm not sure my wife would have reacted the same way." Detective Sergeant Hoover gave a mirthless laugh. "Especially if she found out it hadn't stopped, that you saw Mrs. Davis on the day of her death."

"What are you talking about?" Jackson blanched. "I just told you I stopped seeing her well before she died."

Detective Young pulled a photo from a file. "Then how do you explain this? It's a photo of you arriving in Washington on the same train as Mrs. Davis on the day of her death."

Jackson glanced at the picture and put his head in his hands.

"He's stalling for time. Press him," Mac said.

Detective Sergeant Hoover threw a glare at the camera.

"Mr. Jackson," Detective Young said. "We have your train ticket. You traveled to Kansas City with Mrs. Davis on Thursday and came back together on the Saturday of her death. Why?"

"She asked me to accompany her to see her divorce lawyer."

If he went with Eleanor on Thursday ... "Ask if he met Greg Williams—or Gary Wallace." Mac spoke into the mic.

"Was there anyone else with you on Thursday?"

"Eleanor had a friend with her. I don't remember his name. When he saw me, he made some excuse and went to another carriage."

"Sir, the ID kit is on my desk. Want me to get it?"

"Later. We'll finish here," Detective Sergeant Hoover said.

"Of course."

"Ask if he knows if Eleanor had served divorce papers on Connor before she died," Mac said.

"Had Mrs. Davis served divorce papers on her husband before she died?" Detective Young said.

Mac held her breath.

"Yes, but he hadn't signed them yet. That's why she was back at the lawyer. She wanted to see if there was anything she could do to force him to sign."

"Was there?"

"She hadn't filed with the courts yet. Her lawyer told her Connor was probably dragging his feet, hoping to change her mind—because of the prenuptial agreement. If she filed, he'd have no reason not to sign." Robert Jackson rubbed the back of his neck. "She decided to tell her father about the divorce and ask his opinion first. We came back to Washington, and somebody shot her before she could talk to him."

A chill ran down Mac's spine. Connor Davis killed his wife. But how? She looked at Sam. "What have I done?"

"We're in this together." Sam grasped Mac's hand. "And with God's help, we'll find the answer."

"I think we know the answer." Mac took off her earpiece. "I helped a killer get away with murder."

"Not necessarily." Sam swiveled her chair away from the screen. "Someone may want it to look like Connor did it."

"Why?"

"Think about it." Sam grabbed Mac's arm. "Someone kills Eleanor, assuming Connor will be charged, and he is. But, he's acquitted."

"Okay. Then what?"

"This someone still has it in for Connor, so he decides to ruin his life. What better way than to leak the news that Eleanor was divorcing him?"

Mac stood. "He'd have to know about the prenups."

"Yes."

"Once Mr. Fischer learned Eleanor served papers on Connor, he'd lose his job and any inheritance he might have had." Mac sat and stared at her screen once more. "Robert Jackson told us about the prenups and about Eleanor filing for a divorce."

"Yes." Sam returned her gaze to Interview Room One.

CHAPTER 27

Mac and Sam followed the officer to Chief Baker's office.

"The Chief said to wait here. He'll be back in a minute."

Mac strolled over to the file cabinets. Photos sat among potted plants. One was of an attractive woman and the Chief, another, two young girls, and a third, a family shot showing the same girls as young women with kids of their own.

His daughters were friends with her sisters in high school. They would have known Eleanor, Connor, Robert and Faye Jackson, and Mary Elizabeth. She moved behind his desk to his bookcase.

"Mac, quit snooping. Sit down," Sam said.

"I'm not snooping." Mac straightened from examining a public service award the Chief had received.

"Miss Love, I believe that's my side of the desk." Chief Baker entered, trailed by Detective Young.

Heat climbed Mac's neck. "Yes, sir." She took a seat next to Sam.

"What are your thoughts after observing the interview with Robert Jackson?"

"Sam had an interesting idea." Mac glanced at her partner. "I'll let her tell you."

Sam related what she and Mac had talked about before.

"If your idea about Robert Jackson wanting to ruin Connor Davis's life is true, then he must be holding onto some terrible hatred."

"Or jealousy," Mac said.

"Over Eleanor?"

"Eleanor, the inheritance from her father, the fact that Connor was given a position in the company and didn't have to work hard to build his own like Rob did." Their foolproof idea didn't seem so foolproof anymore.

"But if he loved Eleanor, why kill her?"

"Maybe even though she wanted a divorce from Connor, she still didn't want Rob." Mac pulled at her ear. "I'm not sure."

"It bears investigating," Chief Baker said. "Our priority is to talk to the Kansas City lawyer. What do you and Mrs. Majors intend to do, Miss Love?"

"I think I need to find out if Connor's alibi is as solid as it seemed." Which meant a trip to Kansas City for her as well.

"I'll drop you at home, Sam. There's no need for Alan to come pick you up." Mac unlocked her car.

"What are you going to do?"

"Go back to Miss Ps for the night."

"What about tomorrow?"

Mac turned to face her friend. "I think I'll make a trip to Kansas City and take Dr. Ulrich up on his offer of dinner. If he's available."

"I'm coming with you." Worry etched Sam's face.

"I'm afraid he won't loosen up enough to tell me the truth with anyone else there." Mac creased her brow. "Besides, you're still healing from cracked ribs. It's probably not a good idea for you to travel yet."

"You're probably right." Sam nodded. "So, what can I do?"

"You and Miss P need to get our office up and running again, for one thing." Mac started the car. "And there are a few other things that need checking. We can talk about them tomorrow."

After dropping Sam off, Mac turned her car toward Miss P's and what she hoped would be a delicious dinner. She wasn't disappointed. The tantalizing smells of baked chicken, mashed potatoes, and green beans drifted through the air before she reached the door.

"Miss P, you're going to spoil me." Mac entered the kitchen.

Jake sat at the table. He had on a T-shirt and jeans. He looked good.

Duke sat curled on his lap.

Warmth spread through her. "You're here."

"I am." He chuckled. "Miss P stepped out for a moment. Why don't you sit down?"

She pulled her eyes away and surveyed the three place settings at the table. There was one where Jake sat, one next to him, and one across from him. She headed for the chair across from him.

As she approached the table, Duke hissed at her.

"Hey." Jake tapped him on the back. "Mac's my friend."

The cat jumped to the floor and stalked out of the room.

"So I'm a friend." She couldn't keep the disappointment from her voice.

"I didn't think you were ready for more yet."

"What do you mean?" What was he talking about? Had he found out about Nate?

"You're back. Excellent. We can eat." Miss P bustled into the kitchen and began placing food in serving bowls.

"Let me help." Mac dumped her purse and jacket on a stool and took a platter of chicken from Miss P.

"I heard you and Sam had an exciting afternoon," Jake said.

"Uh huh." Mac sat and placed her napkin on her lap.

"Blessing first, then we can talk about your day, Mackenzie." Miss P folded her hands. "Thank You, Lord, for this food and these dear friends. Amen."

Jake forked a piece of chicken onto his plate and passed the platter to Mac. "I talked to Detective Young before you got here. He told me about your theory."

"What do you think?"

"It's one possibility. I don't think Young had a chance to tell you what he discovered."

"Which was?"

"Connor was also on the train the day Eleanor died. His seat was in a different car."

Mac threw her hands in the air. "Was there anyone who wasn't on that stupid train?"

"Mackenzie." Miss P peered at her over her glasses.

"Sorry, Miss P, but this is so frustrating." She plucked her napkin from her lap and wiped her mouth.

"The strange thing is, he got on in Hermann and off in Kirkwood." Jake took a bite. "Does that make sense to you?"

"He could buy a ticket for Hermann to Kirkwood and get off at Washington." Bitterness filled her mouth. She took a sip of her tea. "The more we investigated, the more I began to suspect his alibi was no good. I'm going to Kansas City and confront David Ulrich."

"Whoa." Jake choked on his drink. "Not a good idea."

"He asked me to have dinner sometime. I've decided it's time." She took a bite, chewed, and swallowed. "And while we're at it, I'm going to convince him to tell me what actually happened that day."

"In that case, I'm going with you."

"Oh great. He's certain to tell all with a police officer there." Mac raised an eyebrow at him.

"Not to dinner, but I am going with you to Kansas City."

He gave her a no-changing-my-mind look, and she knew it was no use arguing. Mac's fingers tightened on her glass. Jake and her on a train for four hours together? Her hunger spiked at the thought.

"Would you pass the green beans?"

"What else was Detective Young able to ascertain?" Miss P dabbed at her mouth with her napkin.

"Did you find Evans? What did he have to say?" Mac spooned more mashed potatoes onto her plate.

Jake caught her eye. "They found Evans. He'd been murdered."

"Oh no," Miss P said. "Not another poor soul."

Mac's throat closed. "What did he know that got him killed? Do you have his reports to Mr. Fischer?"

"They're missing." Jake placed his napkin on the table. "Somebody at Fischer's plant is in this case up to their neck."

"Was Connor there?"

Jake nodded. "At least in the morning. They couldn't find him after the shooting."

"Do you think it was Connor who killed Evans and later shot at us?" Mac searched Jake's face for answers.

He took in a breath and exhaled slowly. "I'm not sure. It's possible."

Rage swept through her. Connor may have fooled her once, but never again. If he killed Evans, she'd make sure he paid.

CHAPTER 28

Fresh energy filled Mac as Miss P's sedan approached their newly renovated office. The morning sun spotlighted the gleaming new windows and fresh paint. Autumn leaves carpeted the grass with brilliant reds, oranges, and yellows.

She itched to get back to normal and solve Eleanor's murder. And Mary Elizabeth's. She'd almost forgotten M.E. Why did she get the feeling they were connected?

"It looks great." Jake opened his car door and withdrew his cane.

"Yes." Miss P turned her car off. "They did an excellent job. Let me help you inside."

"I'm fine." He motioned her away.

Mac stood for a moment, taking it in. She was ready to rock and roll.

Alan drove up with Sam in the front seat. "Nice. Looks better than new."

"I told you." Sam hurried up the walk and turned. "I'll call later, honey. Love you."

Alan blew her a kiss, got back in his car, and left.

Mac unlocked the door and stepped in. She gasped. All the furniture was back in place. How did that happen?

"I called yesterday, and they delivered it while you were at the police station." Miss P drifted throughout the rooms, making minor adjustments. "I believe it is as you had it."

"Yes." Mac managed around the lump in her throat.

Sam joined them. "It's perfect. Thank you."

Boxes of files stood against the walls, waiting to be put away. Mac rubbed her hands together. "Let's get this party started."

"I'll make coffee," Jake said.

As they organized the files, they separated the ones pertaining to Eleanor and Mary Elizabeth out and placed them on the conference table once more.

"I want to talk to everyone before I leave." Mac pulled a chair out and gestured for the rest of them to sit as well.

"Before we leave." Jake sat next to her.

She caught a whiff of his aftershave. What was she going to say? "We've narrowed possible murderers in the Eleanor Davis case to three. Faye Jackson, Robert Jackson, and Connor Davis."

"My money's on Rob Jackson," Sam said.

"He's high on the list."

"We haven't explored the possibility of Mrs. Jackson very far, have we?" Miss P said.

"No. Would you like to do some work on that?"

"Certainly." She made a note on her pad.

"Detective Young may be able to help you there." Jake put his elbows on the table. "He's got information on their train travel."

"Thank you, Detective."

"What about Connor?" Sam stopped typing. "Even if he killed his wife, we can't touch him."

"Unless he killed Evans too." Mac narrowed her eyes at the thought.

"Evans is dead?" Sam paled.

"Yes. He must have seen something." Her temples throbbed.

"We've been so busy with Eleanor's case, we haven't spent much time on M.E.'s murder." Sam sipped her coffee. "I guess we need to do some work there as well." She made a note.

"I know this much. Her husband is the only one of all the suspects who doesn't have a rail pass," Jake said. "If that means anything."

"I think it does." Mac rose and paced. "Either he didn't care enough about M.E.'s frequent trips to Kansas City to follow her, or he paid more for regular tickets to cover his trip history."

"I don't think he had the time or the money to track his wife."

"Me neither. Can Detective Young get records of his credit card purchases for us?" Mac looked at Jake.

He rubbed his jaw. "We'll try, but we're not officially investigating that case."

"I get the feeling that Eleanor's case and Mary Elizabeth's are related by more than just timing." She chewed on a fingernail.

"What do you mean?"

"I'm not sure, but we need to look for connections." Mac turned to her partner. "Can you do that while I check out Connor's alibi?"

"I'll try." Sam made a note, but she didn't sound too hopeful.

"I'll make lunch while the rest of you sort out the files." Miss P stood and gathered the coffee mugs.

Mac picked up a box and headed for her office. She

hummed a tune as she placed folders in her file cabinet. A hint of aftershave, and Jake stood next to her. She dropped the manila folder she was holding, bent to retrieve it, and hit her head on the open drawer. "Ow."

"Let me see." Jake eased her hand away from her forehead. "No bleeding. You'll live." He handed her the file. "Here are your papers."

"Thanks." She shoved the folder between two other files and closed the drawer. "Did you need something?"

"No."

Was he smirking at her?

"Just wanted to let you know that Detective Young will drive us to Kansas City today." He grinned. "We leave right after lunch."

"Fine." Part of her was relieved, and another part disappointed. What was up with that?

Jake gave the cabinet a light tap and left.

JAKE'S strong will kept him from showing the pain he experienced climbing into the passenger's side of the police issue SUV. Once in, he glanced at Vic and Mac before wiping the sweat from his face and neck.

"How's your leg?" Detective Young started the car.

"Good."

"Glad to hear it. I'm surprised the Chief okayed this trip for you."

"He didn't." Jake stared at Vic. "I didn't ask for permission. You okay with that?"

Young gripped the steering wheel. "We never had this talk." He put the SUV in gear and backed out of the driveway.

Jake glanced at Mac sitting behind the driver. She stared

out the side window, wrapped in an afghan with earbuds in place. Had she heard their conversation? Not likely. But it didn't matter.

He took a longer look at her dark hair shining in the afternoon sun, and her profile—long lashes, a straight nose, and full lips. An ache rippled through his chest.

Permission or no. There was no way he was letting her return to Kansas City without him.

"Let me know when we're close." Jake reclined his seat and closed his eyes.

A COUPLE OF HOURS LATER, Mac pulled her earbuds from her ears. "Detective Young? Do you know how to get to my sister's house?"

"Yes, ma'am. I put the address into the GPS."

"Great. You can drop me off and go on to your hotel."

Young glanced at Jake, who remained asleep. "Jake? We're here."

"Jake." Mac touched his shoulder. "Wake up."

He turned to face her. "Hi beau—Mac." The color drained from his face and he powered his seat back up.

Did he almost call her beautiful? Mac swallowed her surprise. "What's the plan for tomorrow?"

"Vic and I will visit Eleanor's lawyer while you have lunch with Dr. Ulrich. Then we'll pick you up at your sister's place and head back to Washington." Jake avoided her gaze.

"Okay. I guess we'll keep in touch by text?"

"Yes." Jake gave her a worried look. "Call if you have any problems."

Detective Young pulled into Kate's driveway and hopped out to help with her suitcase.

"I will. See you tomorrow." She was tempted to add "beautiful" but decided against it. She grinned to herself.

Once inside Kate's house, Mac called David Ulrich. "Just wanted to make sure we were still on for lunch tomorrow."

"Of course. I'm looking forward to it." Ulrich's voice purred across the phone. "Why don't I pick you up at noon?"

"That would be lovely, except I have some errands to run in the morning. Why don't I meet you? My sister can drop me." Mac lowered the timbre of her voice to match his. "Where?"

"The Capital Grille?"

Mac hesitated. She'd never been in there—much too rich for her pocketbook. "What time?"

"Twelve-thirty?"

"I'll see you then."

From the sound of his voice and the choice of restaurant, Dr. Ulrich had ideas about how their lunch would go. An intimate lunch with some wine and who knew what else.

But Mac had her own agenda, and it didn't include alcohol or after-lunch activities. *Too bad, Doctor.*

CHAPTER 29

M ac walked through the double doors of the restaurant into another world—one designed to calm the nerves and slow the pace. Thick carpet, dark wood paneling, and soft lighting from Art Deco lamps combined to create the feeling of being in someone's library.

"When I called to take you up on your invitation, Dr. Ulrich, I wasn't thinking we'd dine at the Capital Grille." Mac slid into the leather booth and smiled at her companion. "At least let's go Dutch."

"Not necessary. And call me David." He cocked an eyebrow at her. "After all, this is our second date."

Mac tensed. "Date?"

"Just kidding." He laughed. "Although, I have to say I was surprised you called. I'd hoped we might spend a quiet evening together, but an afternoon is good too."

"Lunch is all I can manage." She gave him her sweetest smile. "And I'll admit I've got something I'm hoping you can help me with, but it can wait until after we eat." Mac studied her menu. "Everything sounds fabulous. What do you usually order?" She scanned the menu for the cheapest dish. A wedge salad looked good, and if he insisted she order more, the roasted chicken breast.

The server appeared at Ulrich's side.

"Would you like to share an appetizer?" Ulrich raised an eyebrow at her.

She nodded. Why not?

"We'll begin with the lobster and crab cakes." He glanced at Mac.

She gave the server her order, and the doctor finished with his.

"Also, bring us a bottle each of your house white and red wines."

"Very good, sir." The server gave a slight bow.

"Wait." She put her hand up. "I don't drink. Water will be fine." Strike one.

"Make that a bottle of your house red. No white." He folded his arms on the table. "You don't drink. You don't smoke. What vices do you have, Mackenzie Love?"

The serious flirting had begun. "If something is nagging at me, I can't leave it alone until I figure it out, and it drives everyone around me nuts."

"Is something bothering you right now?"

The server slipped their appetizer onto the table between them. David placed a crab cake on a small plate and slid it toward Mac.

"Let's talk about you." Two could play this game. She picked up her fork. "How long have you and your wife lived in Kansas City?"

He chuckled. "Who told you I was married?"

"The mark on your ring finger. I'm a detective, remember?" She gave him the hint of a smile.

"Yes, you are." He wagged a finger at her. "I forget because you're so beautiful."

Their salads arrived.

"I don't think you forget a thing, doctor." Mac looked at him over the rim of her water glass. "But I do think you lied to me."

Ulrich gave her a piercing look. "Maybe we will go Dutch after all."

Mac laughed. "I thought you might change your mind."

"I'm curious. What am I supposed to have lied to you about?"

"You weren't with Connor on the day Eleanor died, were you?"

A twitch at the corner of his eye. But that was all she needed to know she was right. She'd messed up big time.

"Of course I was." He laid his napkin on the table. "I gave my word in a court of law. What more do you want?"

"The truth." She pushed her salad aside. "It doesn't matter now. Connor can't be tried for her murder, but I need to know. Did I get a guilty man off?"

The server brought their meals.

"So that's why you called." David Ulrich stared into his wineglass. "You thought you could flash those gorgeous eyes of yours at me, and I'd confess to you that I'd lied—that I'd perjured myself in court." He gave a low chuckle. "Sorry, my dear, but my testimony stands." He met her eyes with his, open and sincere.

Was he telling the truth now? "Let me ask you this. Do you think Connor hired someone to kill his wife?"

"No." Ulrich lowered his eyes. "He wouldn't have."

"What makes you so sure?" What was she missing?

When Ulrich raised his face to hers once more, sadness filled his eyes. "He still loved her."

And love was one of the main motives for murder.

"Is something wrong with your food?" He indicated her untouched plate.

"No, it's fine." She laid her napkin on the table. "I'm not feeling well."

"I'm so sorry." He signaled the server. "I'll take you back to your sister's place."

"No need. She's coming to get me." Mac stood. "Stay and enjoy your meal."

"I suppose this means no more dates?" He gave her a lopsided grin.

"I don't think so. But thanks for meeting with me." She gave him a brief smile and left.

She hadn't lied to him. The cozy booth now felt claustrophobic, and she longed to be out in the sunshine. The crab and lobster cakes soured in her stomach. Guess they didn't like bleu cheese dressing.

Outside, she crossed the street to wait for her sister.

"What a fool I've been," Mac said under her breath. "I never should have gotten involved with this case."

The door to the Capital Grille opened. David surveyed the sidewalk before stepping outside. Mac shielded behind a tree. He paced in front of the restaurant, his handsome face transformed by anger and his phone pressed to his ear. Wonder who he was talking to? After a moment, he shoved his cell phone into his pocket and strode off.

A text message from Faye dinged on her phone.

saw d n u at capital grille?

Faye was in the restaurant? Why didn't she come over?

Business. Where were u?

lunch with a friend

Mac stared at the text. Something about it looked very familiar. She squeezed her eyes shut in concentration. What was it?

"Sam. Stop daydreaming and get in the car. We need to get back."

"Why? What's happened?"

"Look at your phone, sis."

Mac pulled up her text messages. Before Faye, there were two from Jake. They needed to return to Washington right away.

Mr. Fischer had had a heart attack. The news hit her in the pit of her stomach. She rolled her window down and took a breath of air to combat her nausea.

CHAPTER 30

Mac hugged her sister goodbye and climbed into the rear seat of the police SUV. Jake held his phone to his ear.

"Tell them to check for an injection site on Mr. Fischer," Mac said.

Jake threw her a look that could only be interpreted one way. "Be quiet." She sat back and folded her arms across her chest. That would be the last time she gave him the benefit of her thinking. He would just have to muddle through on his own from now on.

The instant she heard Mr. Fischer had suffered a heart attack, she thought of Mary Elizabeth and potassium chloride. What if his heart attack wasn't natural but attempted murder? It made perfect sense.

When Mr. Fischer possessed proof about the divorce papers, he'd not only fire Connor, but his son-in-law wouldn't be eligible to inherit. Mr. Fischer would have to die before obtaining the divorce decree. Or Connor's life as he knew it was over. He'd be penniless and without a job.

Jake ended his call and turned to face her. "Sorry. I already thought of that, and the doctors are examining Mr. Fischer right now."

"Oh. Good," Mac said. "Were you able to get the lawyer to show you the divorce papers?"

"No, but he agreed to fax them to Mr. Fischer." Jake combed his fingers through his hair. "I think our visit to the lawyer combined with your lunch with Ulrich forced the killer to take action."

"Connor's the killer, and I helped get him off." Mac slammed her fist into the seat in front of her.

"Hey." Detective Young put up a hand. "I'm trying to drive here."

"Sorry."

"I'm not so sure about that." Jake stared out the window. "Remember, his train ticket says he—"

A motorcycle zoomed past them just as Detective Young prepared to pass the car in front. He swerved back into the lane and hit his brakes. "Too bad we don't have the time. I'd go after him."

A memory sparked in her brain. Another motorcycle. Where was it? "What were you saying, Jake?"

"Connor's ticket says he got off in Kirkwood."

"Where Mary Elizabeth lives." Mac pulled her afghan around her. Did he get off in Washington? If not ... but why would he kill M.E.? That made no sense at all.

"What's going through that mind of yours?" Jake tapped his temple. "I can see the wheels turning."

"Total confusion." Mac shook her head. "Who found Mr. Fischer?"

"Connor Davis. But Fischer's assistant said that Robert Jackson was the last to see him alive. He left, and when Connor entered the office, he found Fischer collapsed at his desk."

"Rob? Why would he want Fischer dead?" Mac's head hurt.

"Unless he and Connor are in it together."

"He'll get part of the inheritance money?"

"Possible."

"But you told me Robert's counting on his wife's money, and I can't see him partnering with his rival for Eleanor's affection."

"According to him, they were just friends, and rumor has it Faye's made some poor investments lately," Jake said. "Maybe Robert's pot of gold is shrinking. Or maybe they're all three in it together. I told you the motive smelled of big money."

"I wonder what would happen if Faye thought we were thinking of Connor as her sister's potential killer?"

"You have a devious mind, Mackenzie Love." Jake smiled at her.

"Not really. We owe Faye a visit, anyway." Mac scribbled on her pad. "To give her a report on what we've found so far."

"And stir the pot," Jake said. "One other piece of news. Our thief, Greg Williams, made bail."

MERCY HOSPITAL CAME into view as they crossed over the river into Washington. Somewhere inside, Mr. Fischer fought for his life. Should she stop now or later?

"Drop me at the office," Mac said. "Sam and Miss P will be waiting. I've brought them up to date on what's happened, but we need to discuss our case."

"We'll call you with the latest on Fischer."

Mac grabbed her bags before Young could get out of the car. "Thanks. We'll talk later." As the SUV backed out, she hurried up the walk to the porch.

Miss P opened the door. "Have you heard anything more about poor Mr. Fischer?"

"Not yet." Mac deposited her luggage in her office. "Things are falling into place." She smiled at Sam and sat at the table. "Let's talk about Faye Jackson."

Miss P consulted her notes. "I wasn't able to discover much on Mrs. Jackson, but I happen to have a friend—whom I shall not mention—who told me that Mrs. Jackson and Mr. Fischer are very fond of each other. If you know what I mean."

"I think I understand." Mac chuckled.

"She also said that recently Mrs. Jackson asked Mr. Fischer for a loan." Miss P looked at Mac over the rim of her glasses. "He turned her down, and they had an argument."

"Do you think Rob knew about her money troubles?"

"I doubt it. It seemed she kept her financials separate from his."

"Did he suspect she was having an affair with Mr. Fischer?"

"It's possible. Although I believe it wasn't an affair in the true sense of the word." Miss P removed her glasses. "I think they enjoyed each other's company. They'd meet for lunch or dinner sometimes, but always in public places. Possibly, if something happened to Mr. Jackson, it may have gone further."

"So you don't believe Rob would have enough reason to kill Mr. Fischer based on his relationship with his wife?"

Miss P shook her head.

"What do you think, Sam?"

"I agree." She hit some keys and ran her finger down her screen. "I found out some things about Mary Elizabeth's husband. One of Jake's officers sent me his credit card statements. There are no train tickets on any of them. Based on these results and the fact that he signed the papers for a second autopsy, plus his alibi, I think we can eliminate him as his wife's killer. Despite what Faye thinks."

Mac wrote Connor Davis on her notes and circled his name. Here was the connection she'd sensed all along—the link between the shooting of Eleanor Davis and the poisoning of Mary Elizabeth.

"I think that leaves us with one suspect. Connor Davis may not have killed his own wife, but it appears he killed somebody else's wife. Now we have to prove it."

"But who killed Eleanor?"

"Someone involved with Mary Elizabeth." Light began to shine through the clouds of confusion.

"You mean, it was one of those you do this for me and I'll do this for you type murders?"

"I think so."

Two things nagged at Mac. Faye's text and the motorcycle that sped past them on the way back. She knew if she could puzzle them out, she'd have the answers she needed, but her stomach growled and her head pounded.

"Look at this text I got from Faye." Mac passed her phone to Sam. "Does that seem familiar to you? Or remind you of anything?"

Sam inspected the message. "Maybe if I knew what it said ..."

"It's not what it says. It's the text itself." Mac handed the phone to Miss P. "What do you think?"

"It does seem familiar." Miss P tapped a finger on the screen. The message disappeared. "Oh dear."

"It's okay." Mac shut off her phone. "Think about it. Okay? The other thing that's bothering me has to do with a motorcycle."

"Like the one we saw on the video the day Eleanor returned home on the train?" Miss P said.

"Yes." Mac pointed at her. "That's it. Thank you."

"Of what importance is it?"

"I wish I knew. I only know that my intuition tells me a motorcycle plays a part in this."

"Does anyone involved in the case ride a motorcycle?"

"That's a good question. Would you mind looking into that?"

"Not at all."

"I think we agree that Eleanor's shooting and Mary Elizabeth's murder are intertwined somehow. The main characters seem involved in both. Connor Davis. Faye and Robert Jackson. Even Mr. Fischer's connected to both sets of people." Mac flipped through her notes. "Tomorrow, we call Faye in to report on our progress—and see if we can eliminate her from our suspect list for good."

CHAPTER 31

Q uestions crowded Mac's brain as she drove to work the next morning. She slowed as she neared the office. Something seemed different.

A ray of sunlight illuminated a sturdy fresh sign in the yard. Made of wood and painted to match the house, it announced the offices of Love and Majors, Private Investigators.

Mac sighed. Could they live up to their sign? She'd had no doubts when she and Sam started the business, but would they be able to weave through the tangled web of lies and half-truths of these two cases?

Faye Jackson was due at ten o'clock. Hopefully, she would provide Mac with some answers. She glimpsed the time. A couple of hours until she arrived.

"Miss P, I love the sign." Mac closed the door behind her.

Faye Jackson sat at the conference table, a cup of coffee in front of her. Her silver hair gleamed once more.

Miss P stood behind the elegant woman, arms folded. Her expression reflected how she felt about Mrs. Jackson's early arrival. As mama would have said—"rude, crude, ill-bred, and socially unacceptable." Mac gave her a slight nod of agreement.

"Mrs. Jackson. I didn't see your car."

"It's in the shop. I had my husband drop me off on his way to the office." She lifted her cup. "I hope you don't mind."

"No, of course not. Thank you, Miss Freebody, for making coffee."

"My pleasure."

Mac went into the kitchen and poured herself a mug. Miss P followed.

"When did she get here?" Mac whispered.

"A moment before you arrived." Miss P peered at their visitor over her glasses. "I almost didn't let her in, but that would have been rude."

"Thank you." Mac touched her arm. "We need to let Sam know."

"I managed to call her. She's on her way."

"Can you hold the fort until Sam arrives? I'm going into my office to jot down some thoughts for our interview."

"If I can handle a room full of sixteen-year-old youngsters, I can handle the likes of Mrs. Jackson."

They returned to the conference area.

"I have something to take care of before we talk." Mac smiled at Faye. "I'll be back."

"I'd hoped—"

Mac ignored her protest and closed the door to her office. She took out a fresh pad of paper and prepared an agenda of sorts, listing the information she intended to tell Faye and the questions she wanted to ask her. She was ready. Now she would wait for Sam.

Fifteen minutes later, Alan's car pulled up. Mac opened her door as her partner entered and filled the space with her special kind of sunshine.

"Good morning, Mrs. Jackson." Sam tilted her head at each of them. "Miss P. Mac."

"You're in a good mood, Mrs. Majors."

"I am." Sam tossed her jacket and purse on a chair. "The sun is out, and my cracked ribs are finally feeling better. The doctor said I can start driving myself tomorrow."

Mac put a hand on her arm before Sam broke into dance. "That's great. Can we get to work now?"

"Let me get my computer."

Once seated around the table, Mac gave Faye a serious look. "We began our investigation by examining your brother-in-law's movements over the past six months. And, unless you have fresh evidence, I have to say from what we've found, he didn't kill your sister."

"What did you find?"

"He had no rail pass. Nor did he have any train tickets charged on any of his credit cards. Which points to the fact that he wasn't following her."

"He could have driven or had someone else doing that for him."

"Yes, but if he'd driven, how would he know where she got off? And his bank records show no strange outgoing payments." Mac leaned toward her. "Plus, he willingly signed your request for a second autopsy. If he was guilty, why would he do that?"

Faye ran a hand over her forehead. "I wondered about that myself."

"We've checked his alibi out, and it's solid. He was with their oldest son at the time your sister was killed." Mack held up her hand. "Yes, he could have paid someone to do it, but again, there's no evidence of a payment."

The woman across the table raised her cup with trembling

hands. A drop spilled on her blouse. She stared at it before setting her cup back on the table.

"All these months in my mind, I've cast Mary Elizabeth's husband as her killer. How do I stop?" Faye raised puzzled eyes to hers.

"I'm not sure, but be glad an innocent man wasn't accused of murder."

"Mackenzie, if her husband didn't kill my sister, do you have any idea who did?"

Mac shared a look with Sam.

"Actually, we do, Mrs. Jackson," Sam said. "Connor Davis."

She blanched. "You can't be serious."

"We are." Mac eyed her. Was that disbelief or fear? "He boarded the train that day in Hermann and got off in Kirkwood."

"Just because he rode the train doesn't make the man a killer."

"No," Sam said. "Trust me, we wouldn't be saying this if we didn't have reason to suspect it might be true."

"But why?" She lifted her hands off the table.

"We were hoping you could help us with that part." Mac looked at her notes. "How well did Connor know M.E.?"

"We went to school together, but M.E. was your age. Connor didn't pay any attention to her."

"What about after school?"

"He married Eleanor and went to work for Peter—Mr. Fischer." Faye frowned at her cup.

"I understand you worked for Mr. Fischer at one time and that you're still friends."

"We are."

"I'm sorry. I couldn't hear you."

Faye raised her head. "Yes. Peter Fischer and I are friends. News of his heart attack devastated me."

"Just friends?" Mac said.

Faye stiffened. "Yes, Miss Love, just friends."

Mac glanced at Sam.

"I'm sorry." Sam placed a hand on the woman's arm.

"Losing Eleanor was very hard on him. He loves his boys, but she was his only daughter. He doted on her." Faye pressed her napkin under her eyes.

"I can't imagine what that must be like."

"When Connor was acquitted, he was relieved. To hear that his son-in-law may have killed my sister will ..."

Sam pushed a box of tissues in front of her.

After giving the woman a moment to recover, Mac changed the subject. "How do you know Dr. Ulrich?"

"What does he have to do with this?" Faye's eyes snapped with sudden anger.

"We never know where a vital clue will come from. From your text to me, it was clear you recognized him."

She raised her cup and peered inside. "Could I have another cup of coffee?"

Miss P went into the kitchen and returned with the pot.

"David Ulrich used to practice in St. Louis. He delivered all of M.E.'s babies." Faye folded her hands on the table. "Then, for some reason, he moved to Kansas City."

"Were he and Mary Elizabeth close?"

"If you mean were they having an affair—" Faye's knuckles whitened. "—I don't know."

Mac circled a question mark on her pad and let the silence stretch out.

"I only know I hated the man." For a moment, Faye's face twisted into an ugly mask.

"Why?"

"You can probably guess." She flashed Mac a conspiratorial look. "You've spent some time with him."

"You fell for him, and he broke your heart?"

"He collects them. Broken hearts." She gave a bitter laugh. "The same way some men collect art. But I don't see how this helps prove Connor killed my sister."

Mac doodled the names Connor and David on her pad.

"Were you able to get Mary Elizabeth's cellphone?"

"No. The police have it."

"We'll need to investigate a few more things, Faye." Mac studied her calendar. "Let's set a meeting for the day after tomorrow. We should know more by then."

They stood.

"What do I owe you?" Faye opened her purse.

"Sam keeps track of hours spent. I'll let you talk to her." Mac went back to her office.

She watched through a slit in her blinds as Faye climbed into the passenger seat of her husband's sports car and left.

"You can come out now." Sam rapped on her door.

"What do you think? Is Faye part of a conspiracy to get Connor's inheritance?"

"I don't see it," Sam said. "Those were actual tears over Mr. Fischer."

"And I believe you truly shocked her when you suggested Connor Davis killed her sister," Miss P said.

"I agree." Mac scribbled on her notepad. Connor and David. *cnd. dnc.* She plucked her phone off the table. "Miss P, would you get the screenshot of Eleanor's text message for me?"

"Certainly." She reached for the folder. "Let me see. Ah, here it is."

"Look." Mac spread the paper on the table and laid her phone next to it.

saw d n me xoxo ?

saw d n u at capital grille?

"What do you see?" Mac said.

"They're the same. Except the first says me and the second says you."

"What if the first says M.E., not me?" Mac jabbed at the paper. "The d's are the same—David Ulrich. Mary Elizabeth was having an affair with Ulrich."

"And how does that help us?"

"One person takes care of another person's problem." Mac pointed her fingers and crossed her arms. "Connor killed Mary Elizabeth for David Ulrich and—"

"David Ulrich killed Eleanor for Connor." Sam clapped her hands. "Brilliant."

"But how do we prove it?"

CHAPTER 32

Mac paced. "Especially when they give each other an alibi—" She stopped and snapped her fingers. "—except when I asked David Ulrich about it the other day, he twitched. He wasn't at lunch with Connor the day Eleanor was murdered. Which is why Ulrich made that urgent call once I left him at the restaurant. He had to let Connor know I might be on to them."

And right after that, Mr. Fischer suffered a heart attack. A chill ran down her spine. Where was Connor Davis now?

"If you don't need me, I think I'll go visit Mr. Fischer at the hospital." Mac grabbed her purse.

"I'll go with you." Sam closed her computer.

"I'm only going to stay a few minutes." Mac gave her friend an apologetic smile. The vision of Sam shot in Fischer's parking lot was too fresh. She wouldn't put her partner in harm's way again. Not yet. Maybe not ever again. "Afterward, I think I'll head home to catch up on some housework."

"Okay." Sam sat back down. "Alan and I can go later."

In the car, Mac called Jake. Detective Young answered.

"Detective Sanders is in with the doctor, Miss Love. He's checking his wound."

Mac bit her lip. Should she wait? She gave her head a quick shake. Who knew when Connor might show up?

"As soon as he gets through, meet me at the hospital. It's urgent. I'm going to see Mr. Fischer."

"Yes, ma'am."

Maybe she should wait for Jake and Detective Young to get there, but an overwhelming sense of urgency pushed her to continue on. A storm was brewing. And she was driving straight into it.

MAC STEPPED off the elevator on the cardiac floor of the hospital and headed for the room number she got from Information. An empty chair sat in the hallway outside Mr. Fischer's door. An alarm rang in her mind.

"Excuse me." Mac approached a nearby nurse and showed her credentials. "Where's the officer who was sitting there?"

The young woman in scrubs peered at the empty chair before returning to her charts. "He went into Mr. Fischer's room with the patient's son." She glanced at Mac.

"How is Mr. Fischer doing?"

"Who are you again?" The nurse peered at Mac's I.D.

"I'm working on a case for Mr. Fischer."

She nodded. "His vitals are improving, but we're keeping him heavily sedated." Her phone buzzed, and she hurried down the hall.

A sigh of relief escaped Mac's lips. Thank God. She pushed through the door, ready to greet whichever son had come see his father. Mr. Fischer lay still, wires and tubes connecting him to machines next to his bed. A man stood with his back to Mac on the far side of the room.

"Hello. I'm—" Where was the officer? Apprehension passed over her like a chill breeze.

"Good morning, Mac." Connor Davis turned and strode around the bed, a syringe in his hand.

"What are you doing, Connor?"

"What does it look like?" He grabbed her arm. "I meant this for Fischer, but I can use it on you just as easily."

"Potassium chloride?"

Connor nodded.

"Supplied by Dr. Ulrich. You and your friend, David, traded murders."

"I asked you to drop your investigation." He glared at her. "But not you. Oh no."

She needed to keep him talking. Somebody would come into Mr. Fischer's room soon—a nurse or an aide—somebody.

"Where's the guard? The nurse said he came in here with you."

"He won't be coming to your rescue." Connor inclined his head toward the closed bathroom door. "He's taking a long nap."

Fear clawed through her. Mama's voice sounded in her head.

Trust in the Lord.

"You can't hold on to me and inject Mr. Fischer too." She gave him a frosty look. "What will it be, Connor?"

"Why did you have to keep pushing your nose into Eleanor's murder?" His face reddened. "I gave you so many warnings. David wanted to kill you, but I said no. I told him you'd back off." He squeezed her arm tighter. "But you didn't."

She gritted her teeth in pain. "You'd better act soon, or someone will come in. You know how hospitals are."

"Shut up." He leaned close, sweat dripping down his face.

There was a rap on the door and a man in a white coat slipped inside, closing the door behind him.

Connor jerked her around. He got behind her, encircling her body with his left arm and holding the needle to her throat with his right hand.

"What's going on?" Ulrich glared at Connor Davis. "How did she get in here?"

Connor relaxed his grip. "She knows about us and what we did."

"Give me that." Ulrich snatched the syringe from Connor's hand and marched across the floor. "We'll take care of Fischer and then figure out what to do with her."

Oh no you don't. She drove her elbow backward into Connor Davis. A gust of air and he doubled over, releasing her. She pivoted and brought her knee up under his chin. His head snapped back. Mac seized him by the shoulders.

Ulrich whirled and charged her, syringe held high. Mac thrust Connor between her and the doctor. Ulrich plunged the needle into Connor's back and he screamed.

"You witch." Ulrich bent to wrench the syringe from Connor's spine, but it wouldn't budge.

"What's going on in there?" Two nurses and an aide rushed through the door.

Mac moved to the side of the hospital bed and yanked a chair between her and Ulrich. She had to protect Mr. Fischer.

Ulrich's face contorted into a look of pure hatred. "You're a dead woman." The next instant, he rearranged his features to reflect fear. "They tried to kill Mr. Fischer. Hurry." He pushed through the crowd of people gathered in the hall and disappeared in the confusion.

Hands captured Mac and kept her from running after him.

"He's getting away. We need to catch him." She fought her way into the hall.

The elevator dinged. Jake and Vic stepped off.

"Ulrich tried to kill Fischer." She ran toward the detectives.

Hospital guards grasped Mac by the arms and dragged her back toward Mr. Fischer's room.

"Hold it." Jake blocked their progress. He showed his badge. "What's going on?"

"A man's been murdered, and she ran from the scene."

"I didn't do it." Mac yanked her arms free. "I was running after the murderer." She took a menacing step toward the guards. "But thanks to you, he's got away."

"Easy, Mac." Jake faced the guards. "This is Mackenzie Love. She's been working with me on a case. Show me the dead man." He motioned for Mac to come along.

She trembled with anger and frustration. One more minute and she would have known where he went. Could have followed. Connor was greedy, but David Ulrich … She'd seen his face without the mask.

He was evil.

CHAPTER 33

"What a mess." Jake surveyed the scene in Mr. Fischer's hospital room. Medical personnel had tried to save Connor Davis's life. Puddles of a clear liquid dotted the floor along with cast-off packaging for tubing, gauzes, and syringes. A forensic nightmare.

"At least they didn't get to Mr. Fischer," Detective Young said.

"Thank God for that." Jake ran a hand through his hair. "And Mackenzie. If she hadn't come when she did, the old man would be dead. Where is she?"

"She's in the hall waiting to give her statement."

"How's our officer?" Jake pinched the bridge of his nose.

"A bump on the head. He's being checked out. I think he's more embarrassed than anything."

"He's new. He'll learn."

"Yes, sir." Detective Young gave a slight nod of his head. "We all do."

Jake sighed. "Let's go talk to Mac."

As he pushed through the door, he caught sight of her pacing in front of the nurse's desk. "You're going to owe the hospital for a new floor if you keep that up." He stepped in front of her. "Want to sit down and tell me what happened?"

"What I want is for you to put out an APB on David Ulrich before he gets away." Mac jabbed him in the chest with her finger. "He killed Eleanor and manipulated Connor into killing Mary Elizabeth, and probably Evans. He's pure evil."

Jake rubbed his chest. "Yes, boss."

"Don't 'yes, boss' me." She planted her fists on her hips. "I'm serious."

"So am I." Jake squared up with her and gave her an icy stare. "I know my job, Mackenzie. Now let me do it."

She sat and folded her hands in her lap. "Where do you want me to start?"

"What was so urgent about visiting Mr. Fischer, and why did you want me to meet you here?"

"We'd figured it out. Connor and David Ulrich had swapped murders to confuse the police." Mac picked at her nail. "But when we discovered the prenuptial agreement and the fact that Eleanor had served Connor with divorce papers, they had to act fast. Mr. Fischer had to die."

"The first attempt didn't do the job. So you figured they'd try again."

Mac nodded.

"What aren't you telling me?"

"Before Ulrich left—" Mac raised glistening eyes to him. "—he vowed to kill me."

Jake's chest tightened.

"We've got an APB out on him. I'm betting Ulrich's on his way to Mexico by now." He sat beside Mac and took her hand in his. "Their master plan is in shreds, and there's nowhere he can go. We'll find him."

"I saw the look in his eyes." Mac shuddered. "He's got nothing to lose."

"I'll—"

She put a finger on Jake's lips. "Don't. I know you mean well, but you can't promise to keep me safe."

Jake's throat ached. Mac was right.

"Come on. Let's go to your office." He stood and offered her his hand. "I'll have one of my guys drive your car."

As HAPPENED SO OFTEN in October, the beautiful autumn day gave way to ominous gray clouds. The wind whipped Mac's hair across her face as she walked ahead of Jake and Detective Young into the building. Sam rushed from her office and Miss P from the kitchen.

"We heard on my police scanner about what happened at the hospital." Sam held Mac at arm's length and studied her. "Are you hurt?"

"I'm fine." Mac gently pulled away. "Just tired." She walked to a chair in the reception area.

Sam followed. "At first, we heard that a man and a woman tried to kill Mr. Fischer. Then they said Connor Davis was dead and a man impersonating a doctor fled the scene."

"The APB came through for Dr. Ulrich shortly thereafter," Miss P said. "We then realized that Connor and Dr. Ulrich must have attempted to kill Mr. Fischer, and you were able to save the day."

"Our very own superwoman." Sam clapped her hands together.

Mac flicked her a scowl. "Not hardly. Ulrich got away."

Jake sat at the conference table and peered at his phone. Young stood at the front window and scanned the street.

"Anything?" Mac's pulse spiked as she remembered the look on Ulrich's face.

Jake shook his head.

"Is something wrong, Detective?" Miss P said.

Mac shared a look with Jake. "Before he ran, Ulrich threatened to kill me." A chill went through her.

"Oh, Mac." Sam jumped to her feet and paced. "Why didn't you let me come with you?"

"I wasn't sure Connor and Ulrich would be there."

"But you thought so and were going to take them on by yourself." Sam stopped in front of Mac and folded her arms across her chest. "You were afraid I'd get hurt again, weren't you? What kind of partnership is this when you make decisions for me?"

Sam's angry tone took Mac by surprise. After all, she was only trying to—keep her partner safe. Mac stood. Sam was right. She'd ranted at Jake for doing the same thing.

"I am so sorry, Sam." Mac touched her friend's arm. "Never again. I promise."

"Two are better than one. If one falls, the other can pick you up." Sam unfolded her arms and gave Mac a hug. "You are my best friend as well as my partner. We're in this together."

Mac nodded.

"Ladies and gentlemen, please sit, and we'll have something to eat." Miss P placed a platter of sliced turkey on the table, along with stuffing and carrots.

The woman was a blessing.

As they ate, the sky grew dark, and wind rattled the windows in the small house. The lamps flickered once.

"Time to clean up and head for home." Mac rose and gathered dishes off the table.

"Detective Young, please give my sister a ride home and

stay with her until her husband arrives," Jake said. "We'll go back with Miss P in her car."

"Are you sure? I can wait for Alan to come," Sam said.

"I'd feel better if you went with Vic, sis." Jake placed his hands on Sam's shoulders.

"By the way," Miss P said. "I found out that Connor Davis, Robert Jackson, and Dr. David Ulrich all belonged to the same motorcycle club. That's how they met."

"You say belonged? Do they still ride?"

"It's my understanding from Mrs. Jackson that Dr. Ulrich is the only one who currently owns a motorcycle." Miss P placed her purse on her arm. "I haven't discovered the make yet."

The video of a black motorcycle behind Eleanor Davis as she pulled away from the train depot parking lot played on a loop in Mac's head. Interspersed with clips of the motorcycle that sped past them on the highway coming back from Kansas City.

Could it be the security camera caught Eleanor Davis's killer on tape?

THE GATES across Miss P's driveway shuddered to a close. Mac wrapped her sweater tighter around her as she hurried for the door. The trees surrounding the small patio performed a shadowy dance in the howling wind. Severe thunderstorms were predicted with a possible tornado.

"Do you need help?" Mac took hold of Miss P's elbow.

"I believe I can manage." She held her purse close to her body. "How is Detective Sanders doing with his cane?"

Mac glanced at Jake. He leaned against the car, surveying the darkness. "Are you coming?"

"Be there in a minute."

Stepping inside was like losing her hearing but gaining her sight. Duke materialized at their feet. He rubbed his head against Miss P's legs.

"How are you, my handsome house guest?" She bent to caress his soft fur. "Let's get you something to eat. Some turkey, perhaps?"

"Miss P, you're spoiling my cat." Jake removed his jacket and hung it on a peg near the door.

"*Mrawr.*" Duke looked at Jake with his emerald eyes.

"I'm afraid I will continue to spoil your precious cat as long as he is my guest, Detective. Just as I spoil you." She gave him a sweet smile.

"Yes, ma'am." Jake yawned. "I'm headed for bed. If we have a tornado warning during the night, where's your shelter place?"

"I have a vaulted wine cellar." Miss P eyed his cane. "I think you have improved enough to take the stairs down to it if the need arises."

"I'll scoot down if necessary. In the meantime, I plan on getting some sleep."

"Me too." Mac waved to her friends, turned, and placed a finger on her nose. "If I can find my bedroom."

"I'll take you." Miss P smiled.

The old house creaked and shuddered in the wind. Miss P turned out lights as they climbed the stairs. Nightlights, placed in strategic places, lit their path. Once they reached her bedroom door, Mac bid her goodnight one more time.

"In the morning, use your nose to find the kitchen, and if you have trouble, call me on your phone and I'll give you directions."

Mac laughed. "I may need to do that." She pushed her door shut and prepared for bed.

Rain pelted the window and lightning pulsed in the sky behind the shades, followed by the roll of thunder. Mac climbed into bed and pulled the quilt around her neck. The illuminated dial on the clock read ten pm. She turned over and recited the Lord's Prayer.

CHAPTER 34

M ac woke with a start. Something had changed. Her
heart pounded in her chest. The wind had shifted,
whistling through the treetops outside her window, but that
wasn't what frightened her. She turned over.

No numbers from the clock shone in the darkness. No
nightlights glowed under her door. Had the storm knocked out
the electricity? A flash of lightning lit the room for a second
and she gasped. A shadow stood at the foot of her bed.

She rolled off and crouched between it and the wall.

"I can see you." David Ulrich's voice slithered around her
like a boa constrictor. "I have night vision goggles."

Mac lay on her belly and squirmed under the antique bed.
Where was he? Footsteps sounded on the window side of the
bed. She scooted to the wall side, crawled out, and felt for the
door.

"Help." Mac yanked the door open just as he grabbed her.

He slammed the door and brought his knife to her throat.
She threw her weight backwards against him and they fell to

the floor. Warm sticky liquid ran down the front of the T-shirt she wore to bed.

A high-pitched screech filled the room. The tornado warning sounded on her cellphone. Ulrich's attention wavered long enough for Mac to force his arm away from her neck and roll away. He swung at her, catching her in the forearm with the sharp blade.

She screamed in pain and scooted under the bed again.

"Come out." Ulrich lay on his stomach and started to follow her. His night vision goggles hit the bed frame, and he uttered a curse.

"Mackenzie, we need to move to the wine cellar." Miss P opened the door and shone a flashlight into the room. "What's going on?"

Ulrich leaped to his feet and brandished his knife. "Turn that light off, old woman."

"Miss P, run." Mac slid out from under the bed and grabbed her phone. She hit the flashlight button.

When Ulrich pivoted toward her, she shined it into his eyes. He tore his goggles from his head. A kick to his stomach drove him away from the door. She ran out into the hall and stumbled down the stairs, her legs giving out as she reached the foyer.

Jake picked her up and carried her to a sofa in the den. Footsteps sounded on the stairs behind them.

"He has night glasses." A whisper was all Mac could manage.

Jake nodded and limped away.

DAVID ULRICH HAD MADE a fatal mistake. He'd come back for Mac. Night vision or no, the mad doctor wouldn't get away this time. Jake stood, back against the wall adjoining the hall, and strained to hear past the pounding of his heart.

And there it was. The creak of a board. The man who had hurt Mac moved toward the kitchen. Jake stepped into the hall, switched on his flashlight, and drew his gun. But he'd misjudged.

Instead of several feet apart, the two men were only twelve inches apart. Ulrich swung his knife hand in an arc, knocking the flashlight and sending it flying. Jake ducked and took his finger off the trigger. His flashlight provided enough light to see Ulrich's feet running for the back door.

An angry yowl from Duke filled the air, followed by a scream. Jake snatched his light from the floor in time to see Ulrich yank the cat from his shoulder and fling him across the kitchen. Duke landed on his feet and hissed at the door.

Anger tore through him. Jake heard the revving of a motorcycle engine. "I'm taking your car, Miss P."

He snatched her keys from the counter and ran out into the night. Stinging rain bombarded him as he fought the wind to open the car door.

The big sedan possessed a powerful engine, but was it enough to catch a motorcycle? He had to try. He raced through the gate. The distinct pitch of a motorcycle could be heard in the howling of the wind. Ulrich wouldn't be as familiar with the roads around Washington as he was. That was his only advantage.

If Ulrich wanted to disappear fast, his best bet would be to head for the Highway Forty-Seven bridge. Jake glimpsed a single red taillight. Ulrich had gone the opposite way.

Jake put a call into the station. "I need cars at the intersections of St. Johns Road, Jones Lane, Dunn Springs Road, and Highway T on Old Highway One Hundred. Intercept any motorcycles and take into custody. Armed and dangerous." He gunned Miss P's car down the middle of the road.

The roar of the motorcycle engine grew louder. Had Ulrich turned around, or was this someone else? Jake prepared to intercept. He stopped, blocking the road before the bridge over Dubois Creek, and waited.

A motorcycle raced at him out of the dark. The rider slammed on his brakes and steered the bike off the edge of the bridge into the murky waters below. A high-pitched whine ripped the night before driver and bike flew apart, each landing with a loud splash.

"Need ambulance on One Hundred at the bridge over Dubois Creek," Jake yelled into his phone. "Motorcycle ran off the bridge into the creek."

He reached for his flashlight before jumping from the car and scrambling down the muddy embankment. Rain had swollen the creek into a murderous murky torrent. He played the powerful beam of his light over the swiftly running water. But it was no use. Wind and rain made it impossible to see any sign of either the motorcycle or its driver.

Blue and red lights strobed in the darkness. "Detective." Officers stood on the bridge.

"Shine your floodlights along the banks on either side of the creek." He needed to find David Ulrich—dead or alive.

Jake clamored up to the road and joined the officers. "Anything?"

"We've located the motorcycle, but not the driver."

"Keep searching. He's murdered two people and tried to kill a third." His phone lit up. "Hello?"

"Detective Sanders?" Miss P said. "We're at the hospital. Mackenzie is okay. The wound to her neck didn't hit any major vessels. The doctor closed it with five stitches, but the cut to her arm required ten. I thought you'd want to know."

Jake leaned against the squad car nearby. Her throat cut? And her arm? "I ... thanks for letting me know. I'll be there as soon as I can." When he picked Mac up at the bottom of the stairs, he had no idea. He trembled with fury. "Ulrich better hope someone else finds him before I do," Jake muttered to himself.

CHAPTER 35

"Vic, take over here." Jake tossed Miss P's keys to his Detective. "I'm taking your car."

"Where will you be?"

"At the hospital," Jake called over his shoulder. "Again." He added under his breath.

With lights and siren screaming through the rain-drenched night, Jake experienced a serious case of déjà vu. They had downgraded the tornado warning to a thunderstorm warning, but the wind continued to shake stop signs and blow trash into the streets.

Once again, he found himself in the hospital parking lot, but something was different. The glaring red sign wasn't shining. He pulled close to the entrance and rushed to the doors. They wouldn't open. A nurse inside motioned for him to force them apart. Inside, the lighting was dim.

"We lost power, and the backup generators aren't working properly," the nurse said. "We're using what power we have for critical needs until it's fixed."

"Got it." Jake scanned the waiting room. "I'm here to see Mackenzie Love."

"Follow me."

Jake glanced in the other rooms they passed along the corridor. "Have you had a man come in with suspicious injuries in the last hour?"

"Can you be more specific?"

"Maybe he claimed to have fallen down and to have abrasions and bruises? Possibly a bump on his head."

"No. No one like that."

"If you do, let me know immediately. Please." He flashed her a grim smile.

"Here's Miss Love's room, Detective." The nurse opened the door and gasped.

The hospital bed was empty and Miss P sprawled on the floor moaning. A chair lay on its side and the alarm on the I.V. machine blared. Jake spied Mac's tissue box and ice water jug on the floor under the bed.

"I need help in room twenty-three." The nurse yelled into the hall.

Jake knelt by Miss P's prone figure. "Don't move." He placed a hand on her arm. "Help is coming."

"Nonsense. It's just a bump on the head." She grasped his arm. "Help me sit up."

Jake protested, but she levered herself into an upright position.

"He's dressed like a doctor. He burst in here looking for Mackenzie."

"From the looks of it, she gave him a good fight. Knowing Mac, she could have gotten away from him." *Please Lord, help her get away from him.*

A hospital guard appeared at the door. "Detective, we have a report of a man in scrubs dragging a woman into an operating room."

Jake's heart sank.

"Let's go." Jake raced after the guard into the passage. "Is there a back way to the operating room?"

"The docs have their own stairs. We'll take those."

Jake and the officer hurried up the staircase. He cringed at the echoing sound they made and prayed Ulrich couldn't hear it. At the door, the guard turned the knob slowly and cracked it enough to peer into the doctor's dressing room.

Weak light from the emergency lighting showed an empty room. The guard motioned them forward. Sounds of talking came from beyond the far door. Jake's heart pounded in his chest when he recognized one voice as Mac.

She was still alive, but for how long?

"You still have a chance to get away," Mac said. "Go to Mexico, and from there to one of those South American countries that doesn't extradite Americans."

"You've got it all figured out, don't you?" Ulrich gave a bitter laugh. "Except for the part about money. I counted on my share of Connor's inheritance. You see, I'm broke."

"Broke?" She couldn't keep the surprise from her voice. "You don't act broke."

"I have things and credit." He sighed. "And lots of debt."

"Even so, why risk your life to kill me? What good does that do?"

He tightened his grip on her arm. "It gives me satisfaction."

Sweat trickled down her spine. There would be no talking her way out of this. The man was mad. She examined her surroundings for a weapon. No surgical instruments—no knives of any kind except the one he held against her throat. Every surface was smooth and gleaming.

"They did a nice job sewing your throat wound. Too bad I'll have to undo their stitches."

It was now or never. She slammed her head back as hard as she could into his. He screamed and loosened his grip on her. Blood from his broken nose splattered against her back and neck. She spun away from him and prepared to run.

Jake and the guard erupted into the room, guns drawn. Ulrich dropped his knife to the floor with a clatter and placed both hands over his nose. Mac leaned against the wall.

"Maybe you could save me a little sooner next time?" She slid down to the floor.

"I'll try.

Jake gave her one of those looks—the kind that made her stomach growl. When had she eaten last?

"Your men are almost here," the guard said.

"Take him outside and cuff him to a chair," Jake said. "I'll be there in a minute."

He helped Mac to her feet and inspected her neck. "Not too bad. A little blood. Maybe a stitch or two." He put his arm around her waist. "Let's get out of here."

In the hall, Detective Young and two officers stood by while medical personnel tended to Ulrich's broken nose.

"Have you read him his rights?" Jake said.

"Yes, sir." Young nodded. "And put him under arrest."

"Don't let him out of your sight. I mean it, Vic. Get two men and keep round-the-clock surveillance on him."

"We will."

"I'm taking Mac to get her neck looked at. Keep me posted." He placed his hand on Mac's back. "Let's get you taken care of."

Halfway to the elevators, he heard shouts. Jake pivoted. Ulrich broke free of the police and charged toward them.

"Gun." The shout echoed in the hallway.

Jake pulled his weapon from its holster. "Down." He pushed Mac to the floor.

Ulrich raised a pistol and pulled the trigger. Nothing.

He struggled to chamber a round, and Jake rushed forward. Young and the others grabbed him from behind.

"Sorry, boss." Young retrieved the stolen weapon and handed it back to the guard.

Jake stared at Ulrich. Mac sensed his rising anger. The threatening notes, the office shot up, Mac's car and her bandaged throat and arm, Sam's near-miss.

He cocked his arm back.

She held her breath.

"Don't." Young gripped Jake's bicep. "He's not worth it."

"Vic's right." She laid her hand on the tense muscles in his back and felt them loosen under her fingers.

"Take him away before I change my mind."

CHAPTER 36

J ake took a deep breath. After spending the night in a cell, David Ulrich sat in the interview room, and Jake prayed he could do his job without strangling the guy.

"You going to be all right in there?" Detective Sergeant Hoover nodded toward the door.

"Yes." *Lord, give me Your strength.*

"Let's get to it." Hoover marched inside and took his usual chair. He activated the recorder. "This is an interview with Dr. David Ulrich concerning the incidents this year beginning with the death of Eleanor Davis." He raised his eyes to Ulrich. "At the trial of Connor Davis, you testified that he was with you when Eleanor was killed. Is that true?"

"Now Detective, are you asking me to perjure myself?" Ulrich smirked at them. "Miss Love already tried that, and she's much more attractive than either of you. Although, I must say she has a very hard head." He touched the bandage on his nose. "Do either of you know a good lawyer?"

Jake gritted his teeth. What was it Proverbs said? Something like, "Losing your temper is foolish; ignoring an insult is smart." *Help me be wise and not foolish, Lord.* A calm rose inside of him, and he relaxed.

"If you think she's so attractive, why did you try to kill her —not once, but twice?" Jake moved his chair closer to Ulrich. "Maybe because she found out the truth about you and Connor Davis."

Hatred flickered through Ulrich's eyes. Score one for Jake.

"I don't know what you're talking about. I guess you'll have to ask Connor. Oh, wait." The smirk again. "He's dead."

"But he left a confession with his lawyer to be opened in the event of his death." Jake pulled a sheaf of papers from a file and looked at it. "If there's one thing Connor was, he was thorough." He glanced at Ulrich and then back at the latest Health and Safety report he held in his hand.

"I don't believe you." Ulrich folded his hands in his lap. "Besides, how can his confession have anything to do with me?"

Jake peered at the papers in his hand. "He says you followed Eleanor home from the train station on your motorcycle. Even gives the make and model."

Ulrich grew pale but said nothing.

"You were having an affair with Mary Elizabeth. You wanted to end it, but she threatened to tell your wife." Jake glimpsed the man's white knuckles.

Jake flipped to another page. "You knew Eleanor was divorcing Connor and that serving him papers would ruin his life. So you came to him with a plan. It's all here." He held up the papers.

"You're lying." Ulrich jumped from his chair.

"Sit down, doctor," Detective Sergeant Hoover said.

Ulrich glanced around the room. He plopped into the chair, crossed his legs, and arms.

They were getting to him. Jake studied him a moment.

"Connor also tells how you gave him the potassium chloride and syringe to kill Mary Elizabeth. Now that was a stroke of genius." Jake prayed he hadn't gone too far. "It's clear you were the brains in this duo." He rapped his fingers against the pages. "Connor couldn't have thought of that on his own. It's too clever."

Jake paused and waited.

"He was so weak." Ulrich leaned back and sighed. "I had to hold his hand every step of the way."

"Telling him to intercept the reports from the private investigator Mr. Fischer hired?"

"So easy, but do you think he thought of that? No." Ulrich pointed to himself. "I had to suggest it to him."

"And killing Evans too." Jake put the papers back in his file.

"Of course. He'd seen us in the truck."

"What I don't understand is why you came back for Miss Love. You could have escaped after you put your motorcycle in the creek."

"If she'd left Eleanor's murder alone in the first place, my plan would have worked, and I'd be a rich man." Ulrich's face darkened. "I wanted to get rid of her from the beginning, but nooo. Connor said he'd take care of her." He scowled. "Look what she did to me." He jabbed a finger at his nose. "She deserves to die."

Mac was right. David Ulrich was evil.

MAC LAY in her hospital bed, gazing out the window. The doc insisted she stay one night for observation, and this time, she'd agreed. The storm left behind a clear blue sky, puffy white clouds, and a gentle breeze. She turned away in disgust. Why couldn't the weather match her feelings? Gloomy.

Both their murder cases were finished, and she'd been taking stock. They took on Eleanor's case just because, without pay, and they couldn't count on getting any more money from Mary Elizabeth's either. It didn't sound like Faye had the funds.

Not that money was the most important thing. That's not why they felt called to start the private investigation agency. And solving these murders would help them get future business, but they had bills to pay right now. Like the mortgage, heat, trash, and upkeep on the building. Mac turned away from the window.

They needed more work from paying customers. She touched her neck. Work that didn't involve getting stabbed or shot, preferably. Mac knew what her mama would say.

Trust and pray.

A knock sounded on her door.

"May I come in?" Mr. Fischer walked inside and crossed to her bed.

Mac sat her bed up and straightened her hair. "Sorry. I'm a mess."

"You look fine." The corners of his lips lifted in a gentle smile. "I understand I have you to thank for saving my life the second time."

"I held the fort until the troops arrived. That's all." Warmth crept up the back of Mac's neck and onto her cheeks.

"You and your army—" He smiled again. "—discovered who killed my daughter. For that, I am eternally grateful." He pulled a check from his jacket pocket and handed it to her. "I hope this is enough to show you how much I appreciate all you've done for my family and me."

Mac swallowed as she read the amount on the paper in her hands. She locked eyes with him. "Thank you. You have no idea how much this means to Mrs. Majors and myself."

"I need to go. We're burying Connor this afternoon." He looked at his shoes. "I think he loved Eleanor, but he loved money more. I wish I'd known about the divorce."

"Mr. Fischer, I believe Connor intercepted the reports from your investigator." Mac's brow creased. "And he killed Evans. But the plan began with David Ulrich. He realized that Connor was weak."

"You think Ulrich manipulated Connor into killing Mary Elizabeth while he killed Eleanor?"

"Yes."

"For Eleanor's inheritance." Fischer stared at his hands. "I guess I was a marked man from the beginning."

"I'm afraid so."

Fischer sighed. "So many deaths and so many lives hurt over money."

Mac nodded. "Jake—I mean—Detective Sanders suspected the motive was money all along."

"He's a good man and an outstanding detective." Fischer gave her the same look she got from Sam.

Did everyone think they belonged together except them? Mac smiled. "Yes, he is."

"Goodbye for now, Miss Love."

Mac waved. After the door closed, she picked up the check and dialed Sam.

CHAPTER 37

"It's enough to put a new roof on the office and pay off some of our bills." Mac's heart filled with hope as she told Sam about her visit with Mr. Fischer.

"That's terrific." Sam's joy traveled over the phone. "We're rocking and rolling, partner."

"Finally."

"How are you? Can you come home today?"

"I hope so." Mac shifted in the hospital bed. "These are the most uncomfortable beds."

"You sound good. Not hoarse or anything."

"My throat's a little sore, but not bad." Mac swallowed. "I guess I'd better go. I'll let you know when I get released."

"Talk later."

Mac held the check to her chest and closed her eyes. *Trust and pray.* "Thank You, Lord."

A quick rap on the door and it opened. "Miss Love, I'm sending you home." The doctor strode in followed by two nurses. "Promise me you'll stay out of trouble."

"Not possible, doc." Jake came into view behind the nurse and smiled at her.

Mac's stomach churned.

The nurse slipped the blood pressure cuff on her arm and placed the oximeter on her finger.

"I'll be waiting in the hall. I'm taking you home." Jake winked at her.

Her pulse spiked. Mac scowled at him. He did that on purpose.

JAKE CHUCKLED as he pushed through the door into the hallway. He shouldn't have messed with her, but he couldn't resist.

Besides, seeing her with the bandage around her throat and the one on her arm made his chest ache in a way he'd only experienced once before. He needed to know she was okay, and her scowl showed him he could relax. If he could get a rise out of her, he knew she was all right.

The door to Mac's room opened, and the nurse came out. "You can go in now."

When he entered, Mac stood, brushing her long dark hair. She caught him watching her in the mirror.

"I look terrible."

"You look ... great." Jake tore his eyes from her and scanned the room. "Anything I need to carry to the car?"

"Nope." Mac picked up her purse. "I waived the wheelchair so we can go."

They walked to Jake's car in silence. Once inside, he looked at her. "Home?"

"I should go home." She glanced at him. "But I'd really like to go to the office."

"Somehow, I thought you'd say that." Jake turned right out

of the parking lot. "We interviewed David Ulrich, and you were right. He masterminded the killings of Mary Elizabeth and Eleanor Davis."

"Somehow, that doesn't give me a lot of satisfaction."

"I understand." He reached for her hand and gave it a quick squeeze. "But, the Chief said to tell you many thanks. You helped clear up three murders for him."

"Three?"

"Don't forget Evans, poor guy. He was in the wrong place at the wrong time." Jake flicked a look at her. "Why so glum?"

"I don't know. I guess it's just the letdown from being so active to having nothing to do."

"Not true." Jake turned on his blinker. "There's still one case left to close."

Mac gave him a curious look. "And what would that be?"

"The burglaries." Jake glanced over his right shoulder and changed lanes. "Greg Williams made bail."

"I remember. So?"

Jake pulled up in front of her office. "His hearing was today and he missed it. He's disappeared."

"Did his wife come get him?"

"The Kansas City police put a watch on her right after we charged him. She hasn't gone anywhere."

"Do Sam and Miss P know yet?"

"No. Let's go inside." Jake got out and opened her car door. He took her elbow, and a sensation of warmth spread through his body. "Mac, I care about you."

"I know." She slipped her elbow from his grasp. "I care about you too. I get it. We're friends."

But she didn't get it. He started to say more.

She turned to face him.

He felt his lips drawn to hers.

"Mac." The front door opened, and Sam and Miss P rushed out to greet their friend. "Get in here."

Jake trudged after the women. Why did he keep getting interrupted? He sighed. Maybe it was for the best. He took a seat at the table.

After the conversation calmed down and Mac told her story, Jake cleared his throat. "Ladies, I still need your help. Like I was telling Mac, Greg Williams has skipped bail. We—at least I—think he's still in the area, but I'm not sure where."

"Why would he stick around?" Sam hugged herself.

"Good question." Jake rubbed the back of his neck. "Unless he's planning another job?"

"That's ridiculous." Miss P huffed. "He's already in enough trouble. Why would he consider robbing someone else?"

"Unless he wants to get enough money to leave the country." Mac pulled her notepad in front of her. "What could he be after that would make him that much cash?"

"It would have to be small. Easy to carry and hide. What's he stolen in the past?" Sam said.

"Let me see." Miss P left the room. She returned with a piece of paper and sat once more. "A porcelain statuette was first. The jeweled egg from Mr. Fischer, a Russian meteorite of all things, a string of pearls, and the ruby ring from the family in Warrensburg."

"Wow. That's quite a list." Mac finished writing and sat back. "The thing is, other than Mr. Fischer, he probably doesn't know who has what here in Washington."

"Do you think he might try another robbery at Mr. Fischer's house?" Sam looked at her brother.

"He might. I'll get some men over there." Jake pushed away from the table and walked into his sister's office. "Chief, we have an idea about Williams."

"What is it?"

"He may hit the Fischer mansion again. Let's put some men out there."

"I'll send a couple, but I think it's a waste of time. Williams has charmed some other woman into giving him a ride out of town."

"Yes, sir." Jake pushed End and joined the women. "The Chief is sending a couple of officers to the Fischer house. But he thinks Williams is gone."

"Why do you think he's still around?" Mac stopped pacing and looked at Jake.

"Just a hunch." Jake ran his fingers through his hair.

"Maybe he's lying low for now."

Sam nodded. "That would make more sense. It's less risky than pulling another job."

"Okay. So where could he hide out?" Mac unfolded a map of Washington on the table.

"We've already looked in the usual places—sheds, barns, abandoned buildings," Jake place his finger on the map. "The fairgrounds."

"The old waterworks building in Rennick Park?"

Jake nodded.

Mac stared at the map. If she were on the run, where would she go? Jake had named most of the places that came to mind. She needed to think like Greg Williams. What did he know about Washington? Who did he know? The Fischer factory? Mr. Fischer's home?

And, of course, Eleanor.

Mac's pulse quickened. "Is Eleanor's house vacant? Did you check there?"

"No." Jake sprang to his feet, his phone in his hand.

CHAPTER 38

"What do you think of this color for our roof?" Mac pushed her computer around so Sam could see the screen.

"I like it." Sam clicked on the photo. "Are these architectural shingles?"

"I don't know." Mac pulled her computer back in front of her. "Do you think we should spend the money for those?"

"Let's see what the price difference is. The guy's coming out tomorrow, right?"

Mac nodded.

Sam reached for her phone and scrolled to text. "Good news. The police found Greg Williams."

"Where?" Mac closed her computer.

"Holed up in Eleanor's house." Sam grinned at her. "Just like you thought."

"Yes." Mac fist pumped.

"Jake wants us to meet him at Cowan's for dinner."

"I'm not sure I'm ready for Cowan's yet." She touched the bandage at her throat. "And what if they still hold a grudge?"

"They won't. Besides, you'll be with me and Miss P and Jake." Sam placed a hand on her arm. "But I didn't think about your injuries. I'll call Jake and tell him we can't come."

"I guess I could get some soup," Mac said. "I need to eat something." She squared her shoulders. "Don't call him. We'll stick with the plan."

MACKENZIE FOLLOWED Sam and Miss P into Cowan's restaurant. Jake caught up with them at the door. The new server greeted them, and as she showed them to the corner booth, people at the other tables smiled and nodded at Mac. A few even said hello and called her by name.

By the time they sat down, Mac fought to keep from crying.

"Are you okay?" Jake's warm voice flowed over her.

She nodded and covered her face with her hands.

Jake moved onto the seat next to her and put his arm on her shoulders.

She stiffened, but the warmth from his body drew her in, and she yearned to move into the comfort of his arms. She edged away instead. This place was way too public.

He removed his arm from her shoulders but stayed next to her.

"I hate to do this, but I'm not feeling so good," Sam said. "I think I better leave."

"Oh, dear." Miss P put a hand on Sam's forehead. "You're burning up. Let me drive you home."

"Maybe we should all go." Mac picked up her purse. "We can do this another time."

"No." Sam raised a hand. "I'd feel terrible if I spoiled the evening for everybody. You two stay. Please."

"Fine." Mac laid her purse down. "I'll call later to check on you." What was Sam up to?

After her friends were out the door, Mac turned to Jake. "Tell me you didn't put her up to this."

"No." He gave her a wry grin. "She thought of this one all on her own. Or she may have had help from Miss P."

"You know what I'd really like?" Mac said. "A large chocolate milkshake from Sonic."

Jake grinned. "Me too. Let's go."

Mac waited for Jake on the sidewalk outside the restaurant as he left a tip for their waitress. Poor woman. Her table of four just up and walked out.

The usual clouds and wind hadn't appeared tonight. Instead, a soft breeze played with Mac's hair and stars shone above the buildings. She caught a whiff of his aftershave before she felt Jake's hand on her arm.

"Ready?"

She nodded.

They strolled down the sidewalk through the patterns of light and shadow created by the streetlights. Jake's car was parked half a block away.

"Why is it other people always think they know what's best for our lives?" Mac sighed.

"You mean like tonight?" Jake stopped. "With what Sam did?"

"Yes. She's always telling me how we should date. Even though I keep saying you're the one who said we're friends. Why is she trying to make it more than it is?" Mac grimaced. "That didn't come out right. I didn't mean it the way it sounded."

"How did you mean it?" Jake stepped closer to her. "Because I've been trying to tell you how I feel, and I keep getting interrupted."

Mac stiffened. "I thought—"

"You thought wrong." Jake pulled her into his arms and pressed his lips to hers.

Heat curled down her spine, sparking every nerve in her body. She slid her uninjured arm around his neck and moved closer.

"That's how I feel." He let her go. "I can't make it any clearer than that. What about you?"

Her attraction to him was strong, but was it chemistry or something deeper? She'd been on her own for so long. Was she brave enough to be vulnerable? To discover how she felt?

She stepped close to him and placed a hand on his chest. "This is hard for me."

"I know." He slid an arm around her waist.

She touched her lips to his—gentle at first and then more urgent. After a time, she lay her head on his chest. "I'm starving."

A laugh rumbled through his chest. "Do you want to go back to the restaurant?" He pulled his phone from his pocket and glanced at the screen.

"The milkshake will do." Mac stepped back and smiled at him.

His face turned grim.

"What's wrong?" The wound to her neck throbbed as her heartbeat ratcheted up.

Jake's stomach knotted. "Mom. What's wrong?"

"Son, your father's gotten much worse in a very short time."

A pain stabbed Jake's chest. "What do you mean?"

"He's argumentative, and I'm unable to handle him any longer." Her voice faltered.

Mom'd been so strong throughout his father's illness— never complaining. Not once did she ask for help, and when Jake offered to come spend time with her and dad, she kept saying no. But this was different. He could hear it in her voice.

After a moment, she gave a shaky sigh. "I wonder if you and your sister would help me find a good place for him. I don't want to make this decision on my own."

"Sure. I'll be there as soon as I set things up with the Chief." Jake ran his fingers through his hair. "Have you talked to Sam?"

"Not yet. I'm going to call her next."

Jake ended the call and put his phone in his pocket. His mind whirled with preparations.

Mac touched his arm. "What is it?"

"It's my dad." He raised his eyes to hers. "He's gotten worse and mom needs our help."

Her chestnut eyes grew moist. "I'm so sorry, Jake." She wrapped her arms around him.

"Mac, I ..."

She placed a finger on his lips. "Go home and get ready. I'll call Miss P for a ride."

"No, I'll take you home." He opened the car door for her. "I'll need to talk to Sam and the Chief and make other arrangements."

When he pulled up to Mac's house, he didn't remember the drive there at all. His mind had been preoccupied with thoughts of what he needed to do. He glanced at Mac. Had he said anything to her? He didn't think so.

At her door, he wrapped her in his arms. "When I get back, we'll go on a real date. Dinner and movie or whatever you want."

"Don't worry about that now." She looked at him. The porch light reflected off her glistening eyes. "Your family needs you."

He ached to stay here with her—and yet his heart was breaking for his parents in Florida.

"Come with me," he said.

"You know that's not possible." Mac gave him a sad smile. "Your mother needs you and Sam." She disentangled herself and gave him a gentle push. "Now go. I'll see you when you get back."

He drew in a breath and let it out. "I'll call."

CHAPTER 39

Mac studied the calendar on her phone. Jake and Sam had been gone two weeks, but it felt like a month. Their dad fell and ended up in the hospital for a few days, delaying the hunt for a permanent home for him.

Duke came into her bedroom and rubbed against her legs. She picked him up.

"I know. You miss Jake. I do too." Mac scratched his head. "He'll be back soon. How about chicken for breakfast?"

"*Mwarw.*"

"You are a handsome kitty."

The gray cat turned on his back and pawed her hand.

"You want your tummy rubbed? You've never done that before." Mac stroked the soft white fur of Duke's belly. She laughed. "Well, well, well. Your owner isn't too observant, is he? You're a Duchess, not a Duke. No wonder it took you a while to warm up to me. You were jealous."

A loud purr rumbled from the contented cat.

"I'm glad we're friends." Mac hugged Duchess to her chest and headed for the kitchen. "Us girls got to stick together."

Private Investigator Mackenzie Love stepped into Cowan's Restaurant out of the blustery autumn wind. Greetings and nods from her friends and neighbors warmed her soul.

Ivy hurried over. "I told you they'd get over it." She led Mac to a corner booth. "Your usual?"

Mac nodded, a big grin splitting her face. She looked with fondness at the people sitting around her—her friends and neighbors. Her hometown. A sigh of contentment escaped her lips.

"Have you heard from Jake?" Ivy poured her a cup of coffee and laid two creamer packets on the table.

"I talked to him this morning."

"And?" Ivy perched on the seat across from Mac.

"They found the perfect place for their dad. He and Sam should be coming home in a few days after they finish moving him in."

"Great." Ivy stood. "I know you miss him. And Sam, of course."

Mac nodded. She did miss Jake. Memories of the last night they spent together filled her daytime hours and his kisses sweetened her dreams. So why was she so anxious at the thought of seeing him again?

She knew the answer before she asked herself the question. She was afraid. Afraid of making a mistake. Were her feelings for Jake the beginnings of love or purely physical?

The answer was simple when she'd dated Nate the hippie in college. Physical. They lived day to day and didn't think about the future. When they graduated, she went her way, and he went his.

But it was different now. She wanted more from a relationship, but she knew what it was like to love someone and lose them. Images of her parents filled her mind. And the thought of going through that again scared her.

This was a mystery she couldn't solve on her own.

Lord, help me out here. Help me figure out if what I feel for Jake is love or something else. Please, give me a sign. Something.

She scanned the room once more, hoping to see something that would point to an answer.

Miss P entered with a man behind her. Spying Mac, she headed her way, trailing her companion.

"Mackenzie, I'm sorry to interrupt your breakfast, but I wanted to bring my nephew to see you. He's a lawyer and has decided to practice in Washington." She stepped aside. "Nathaniel Xander Westcott the Third. He tells me you two were friends in college. I was hoping you'd show him around and introduce him to some of your friends."

The good-looking man in front of her was clean-shaven with a smile full of gleaming white teeth and smoky gray eyes that held a wicked gleam.

Mac's mouth dropped open. "Nate?" Mama's words echoed in her head. *"Be careful what you pray for."*

"Good to see you, too, Macky," he said.

"Close your mouth, dear," Miss P said. "It's very unbecoming."

THE END

AUTHOR'S NOTE

In my first series, Trouble in Pleasant Valley, I fabricated the town of Pleasant Valley and placed it an hour outside of Cincinnati, Ohio. Doing that gave me leeway to construct the small community the way I wanted.

But being from St. Louis, Missouri, I grew up with the two big rivers that border it, the Mississippi and the Missouri. And I've always been drawn to the small towns that sit on the banks of the Missouri between my hometown and Kansas City.

Especially Washington, Missouri. About an hour from downtown St. Louis, Washington is an exciting little town with something going on practically every weekend. It's also the first stop for the Amtrak train called the Missouri River Runner which stops twice—once on its way to Kansas City and once on its way back to St. Louis.

I decided to set my new series, Mac and Sam Mysteries, in Washington. Which was not any easy decision. Some places are real. There is a terrific restaurant named Cowans, and they do specialize in mile high pies.

But while you may recognize some buildings, I changed the

269

names. And some places do not look anything like what I describe in the book, like the house on the corner of 2nd and Jackson that is Mac and Sam's office.

I pray I haven't stepped on anybody's toes or hurt anyone's feelings in writing this book. If so, please let me know. Any mistakes are entirely mine.

I want my readers to see the town of Washington as I do—a great place to live.

ABOUT THE AUTHOR

When Debbie Sprinkle retired from teaching in 2004, she had a plan for keeping busy. Attend the women's Bible study at her church, join a local book club, and write a mystery novel. She began going to Bible study on Wednesday mornings, and when her local library started a book club, she was one of the charter members.

One thing led to another—as they usually do—and pretty soon she was a Bible study leader and facilitating the book club. (She says it's because she has the biggest mouth!)

In 2009, she was asked to attend the She Speaks Christian Writers' Conference put on by Proverbs 31 Ministry, where she met Kendra Armstrong. It was their friendship that led to her first book written in collaboration with Kendra, *Common Sense and an Uncommon God*, published in 2012 by Lighthouse of the Carolinas. The second edition was later released under the title of *Exploring the Faith of America's Presidents*.

After attending lots of conferences, taking many classes, and sitting at the feet of a plethora of experienced writers, Debbie wrote her first novel. And, in 2019, her dream came true when *Deadly Guardian* made its debut. Two more novels rounded out the Trouble in Pleasant Valley series, and Debbie is now working on a new set of romantic suspense novels set in a small town in Missouri.

Originally from St. Louis, Debbie received her bachelor degree in chemistry from the University of Missouri-St. Louis. She worked as a research chemist for many years at both St. Louis University Medical School and Washington University Medical School. In 1991, she and her family moved to Memphis, where Debbie taught chemistry for ten years at a private girls' school before retiring.

TROUBLE IN PLEASANT VALLEY SERIES BY DEBORAH SPRINKLE

Silence Can Be Deadly

Trouble in Pleasant Valley

Book Three

It started with a taxi ride ... or did it?

Forced from the career he loved and into driving a taxi, Peter Grace had grown accustomed to his simple life. Until one night when a suspicious fare and a traffic jam blew it all apart, and he was on the run again. Only this time it wasn't a matter of changing occupations but of life and death.

He needed help and he knew where to find it. His old friend Rafe in

Pleasant Valley. What he didn't count on was finding not only the help he needed but a community of new friends and the love of his life. Zoe Poole.

The story of Captain Nate Zuberi and his wife Madison continues as they too risk their lives to help Peter. Along with Peter, Rafe, and Zoe, they strive to catch an assassin.

But can the group of friends find the killer before anyone else gets hurt?

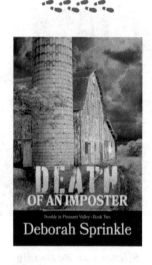

Death of an Imposter

Trouble in Pleasant Valley

Book Two

Her first week on the job and rookie detective Bernadette Santos has been given the murder of a prominent citizen to solve. But when her victim turns out to be an imposter, her straight forward case takes a nasty turn. One that involves the attractive Dr. Daniel O'Leary, a visitor to Pleasant Valley and a man harboring secrets.

When Dr. O'Leary becomes a target of violence himself, Detective

Santos has two mysteries to unravel. Are they related? And how far can she trust the good doctor? Her heart tugs her one way while her mind pulls her another. She must discover the solutions before it's too late!

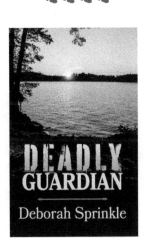

Deadly Guardian

Trouble in Pleasant Valley

Book One

Madison Long, a high school chemistry teacher, looks forward to a relaxing summer break. Instead, she suffers through a nightmare of threats, terror, and death. When she finds a man murdered she once dated, Detective Nate Zuberi is assigned to the case, and in the midst of chaos, attraction blossoms into love.

Together, she and Nate search for her deadly guardian before he decides the only way to truly save her from what he considers a hurtful relationship is to kill her—and her policeman boyfriend as well.

ALSO BY DEBORAH SPRINKLE

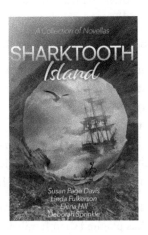

Sharktooth Island

A collection of Romantic Suspense novellas

A fabled island that no one dares to tame.

This collection contains four novellas:

Book 1 - Out of the Storm (1830) by Susan Page Davis

Laura Bryant sails with her father and his three-man crew on his small coastal trading schooner. After a short stay in Jamaica, where she meets Alex Dryden, an officer on another ship, the Bryants set out for their home in New England.

In a storm, they are blown off course east of Savannah, Georgia, to a foreboding island. Captain Bryant tells his daughter he's heard tales of that isle. It's impossible to land on, though it looks green and inviting from a distance. It has no harbor but is surrounded by dangerous rocks and cliffs.

Pirates outrun the storm and decide to bury a cache of treasure on this island and return for it later. On board is Alex, whom the cutthroats captured in Jamaica and forced to work for them. Alex risks his own life to escape the pirates and tries to help Laura and Captain Bryant outwit them. Beneath the deadly struggle, romance blossoms for Laura.

Book 2 - *A Passage of Chance (1893)* by Linda Fulkerson

Orphaned at a young age, Melody Lampert longs to escape the loveless home of the grandmother who begrudgingly raised her. Stripped of her inheritance due to her grandmother's resentments, Melody discovers her name remains on the deed of one property—an obscure island off the Georgia coast that she shares with her cousin. But when he learns the island may contain a hidden pirate treasure, he's determined to cheat her out of her share.

Ship's mechanic Padric Murphy made a vow to his dying father— break the curse that has plagued their family for generations. To do so, he must return what was taken from Sharktooth Island decades earlier—a pair of rare gold pieces. His opportunity to right the wrong arrives when his new employer sets sail to explore the island.

After a series of unexplainable mishaps occur, endangering Padric and his boss's beautiful cousin Melody, he fears his chance of breaking the curse may be ruined. But is the island's greed thwarting his plans? Or the greed of someone else?

Book 3 - *Island Mayhem (1937)* by Elena Hill

Louise Krause stopped piloting to pursue nursing, but when money got too tight she was forced to give up her dreams and start ferrying around a playboy who managed to excel during the Great Depression. When a routine aerial tour turns south, Louise is unable to save the plane.

After crash landing, the cocky pilot is stranded. She longs to escape the uninhabited island, but her makeshift raft sinks, and she and her companions are in even worse trouble. Can Louise learn to trust the others in order to survive, or will the island's curse and potential sabotage lead to her demise?

Book 4 - *After the Storm* *(present day)* by Deborah Sprinkle

Mercedes Baxter inherited two passions from her father—a love for Sharktooth Island, a spit of land in the middle of the ocean left to her in his will, and a dedication to the study of the flora and fauna on and around its rocky landscape.

For the last five years, since graduating from college, Mercy led a peaceful, simple life on the island with only her cat, Hawkeye, for company. Through grant money she obtained from a conservancy in Savannah, she could live on her island while studying and writing about the plants and animals there. Life was perfect.

But when a hurricane hits the island, Mercy's life changes for good. Her high school sweetheart, Liam Stewart, shows up to help her with repairs, and ignites the flame that has never quite died away. And if that's not enough, while assessing the damage to the island, they make a discovery that puts both their lives in danger.

Scrivenings
PRESS
Quench your thirst for story.
www.ScriveningsPress.com

Stay up-to-date on your favorite books and authors with our free e-newsletters.

ScriveningsPress.com

CPSIA information can be obtained
at www.ICGtesting.com
Printed in the USA
JSHW050140080822
29014JS00003B/10